It Happened in Gastown

Melanie Robertson-King

King Park Press

Published by King Park Press

Copyright © Melanie Robertson-King, 2019

Images from Shutterstock, Inc.
(Signed model release on file with Shutterstock, Inc.)

It Happened in Gastown is a work of fiction. Names,
characters, places and incidents are the product of the author's
imagination or are used fictitiously. Any resemblance to actual
events, locales or persons, living or dead, is purely
coincidental.

ISBN: 978-1-9994257-5-3

DEDICATION

For Chris and Wendy – my fellow Princesses of Pandemonium. Thank you for your encouragement and support as well as times together, which include antics, tomfoolery, nonsense, mayhem, and the quest for the perfect body-dump location.

DEDICATION

ACKNOWLEDGMENTS

Thanks to everyone who put up with my daft questions during the research of this novel. Without your help, the book would not have come to fruition.

Huge thanks to my beta-reader, and cheerleader, Joan Edwards. You suggested alternate wording to eliminate unnecessary repetition, told me if things needed further explanation.

If I've missed any member of my team by name, I apologize.

As always, special thanks to my husband, Don, who continues to support and encourage me, and provides a shoulder to cry on when things don't go well. He took me to and from Vancouver by train so I could research the area and get a flavour of the city, and especially the Gastown neighbourhood.

One

Cambie Street, Gastown, Vancouver

Out on routine patrol, Constables Hilary Dunbar and her partner Lukas Stephanopoulos drove north on Cambie Street towards the Gastown Steam Clock. As they passed the end of Blood Alley, she shouted, "Back up. Something's down there."

"Your imagination getting the better of you again?" He teased, but pulled over to the curb and slowly reversed until they blocked the mouth of the narrow passage.

Originally they called the lane Trounce Alley. Some maps still referred to the laneway as that. Others labelled the back street Blood Alley. Given the appearance, Hilary thought the latter more appropriate.

Window down, she trained the beam from the powerful spotlight mounted on the cruiser's mirror into the alleyway. "See, beyond those dumpsters."

"Likely just garbage."

"Wait here; I'm going to take a closer look."

Before exiting the car, she plucked a pair of nitrile gloves and the naloxone kit from the glove compartment. Once out, she shoved them in the pockets of her trousers. With the fingertips of her right hand brushing her gun holster and gripping the barrel of the torch in her left, she sidled towards the object.

Graffiti tags covered the walls of the buildings as well as the wooden hydro poles. The farther into the confined space she crept, the hairs on the nape of her neck bristled beneath the bun in which she styled her black hair. Whatever was down there wasn't rubbish, as Luke said. The pong of stale urine made her eyes water.

Past the second dumpster, the body of a young man leaned against the wall. Dishevelled and filthy, his body odour was strong enough to make the foulest of skunk spray seem mild. At first glance, he appeared dead. His skin had a bluish tinge, and weeping sores dotted his face. Dark circles surrounded his eyes. Inching forward, Hilary squatted beside him.

A blood-filled syringe protruded from his left arm. Flashlight held under her chin; she donned the synthetic rubber gloves she brought with her and felt his neck for a pulse. The rhythmic throbbing beneath her fingertips, barely discernible.

The naloxone. The kit had been made available to officers who wanted the medication. Luke was against carrying the opioid blocker in the cruiser, but Hilary persuaded him. Now was the time to use it. She took the package out of her other trouser pocket, peeled the wrapper open and placed the nozzle in the victim's left nostril and pressed the plunger.

She keyed the mic on her handset and started to speak. "Constable Dunbar." As though on cue, the nearby Steam Clock began whistling — no sense in trying to outperform the contraption. Wait for the completion of its proclamation of the top of the hour — Westminster chimes followed by singular whistle blasts counting out the time. Soon relative quiet returned and Hilary tried again. "Constable Dunbar. Badge 8652. I need an ambulance at Blood Alley and Cambie Street. Suspected drug overdose. Have administered four milligrams of Narcan nasal spray. No response as of yet."

By now, Luke had the cruiser's roof lights on. Blue, red and white alternating then running from the driver's side to the passenger's side of the vehicle.

The wail of the siren grew louder. In minutes, paramedics

jumped out and trundled a stretcher and medical equipment to the stricken person.

Hilary stood back, letting them do their jobs. "I gave him Narcan," she said, handing the spent plastic bottle to one of them.

"He's alive ... just. You found him in time. We've bagged the needle so they can run tests on the contents at the hospital. Figure out what he shot into his veins."

A soft, feminine hand touched his neck. Even though it was gloved, he knew it belonged to a woman. An angel? Had he died? The scent of perfume permeated the air. Not overpowering, but mild and flowery with a hint of patchouli. Far more pleasing than the horrible smells he inhaled before. The person's voice was easy on the ears, and the words were uttered with authority, although he couldn't understand them.

Doors squeaked open. Something landed on the ground with a metallic thud. Footsteps grew louder. Muffled voices spoke around him but not to him. He wanted to shout, 'I'm alive,' but paralysis prevented him. He was conscious of everything going on around him.

A tourniquet tightened around his upper arm. Fingers slapped his inner arm near his elbow. Trying to find a vein. Hopeless. He abused his blood vessels for years, shooting heroin into them. A needle pricked in that area, and the fluid rushing through the syringe stung. Buttons popped, and the cold disc of a stethoscope touched his chest. Someone adhered sticky pads to his torso.

For a moment, his hearing cleared, and he was able to determine what the disembodied voices said.

"Likely a heroin overdose. I'll give the casualty a shot of Narcan," a male voice said.

Something else rushed into his veins.

"The stuff should be working, but it isn't. I don't dare inject another. Can't be an opioid, or it's been cut with something which is keeping him from responding."

"Best get him to emergency. Let them deal with whatever

it is," another man said. This one's voice was lower.

He was weightless. Flying. The next minute he was on his back, something between his lower legs. Beep. Beep. Beep. The irritating sound originated near his feet.

The stretcher bounced and came to an abrupt stop. Must be at the back of the ambulance. The paramedics lifted the gurney and shoved the narrow bed inside. Safety boots tromped on the floor then the backdoors slammed shut. A rubber seal of an oxygen mask pressed on his face; its strap wrapped around behind his head. He was smothering. Unable to breathe. Within seconds, a rush of fresh air tickled his nostrils. Soon after, another door closed, and the engine started.

Hospital. They were transporting him to Vancouver General.

Hilary walked to the back of the ambulance and waited while the paramedics crammed the stretcher into the back. Once the victim was loaded, one EMT climbed in that end. The other got behind the wheel, pulled a U-turn and raced off in the direction of Vancouver General.

"Looks like we're off to the hospital," she said, dropping into her seat and fastening the belt.

"Great. More misspent time and a ton of paperwork because of a drug addict," Luke complained.

"That drug addict is someone's kid," she snapped, her thoughts turning to her friend who died of an overdose.

"Ooh ... aren't we touchy? Turning soft, are you? Biological clock ticking?"

Siren wailing, they sped through the streets. The stretcher bounced against the interior wall as the vehicle sped around corners and hit bumps and potholes. More than once, the driver hit a button, and the alarm yelped. Other times, what sounded like the air horn on a transport echoed through the confined space. Idiots not moving aside to let them pass.

If he died en-route to the facility, he swore he would come

back and haunt the person responsible for not yielding to the ambulance.

Luke put the Dodge Charger in gear and turned the car around, mumbling the entire time. Most of the time, he loved his job but had no use for addicts and their habits. Hilary's reaction caught him by surprise. He knew his partner well, or so he thought. This seemed unlike her. Was there a skeleton in her closet she wanted to keep hidden? He wouldn't press for now, but he would find out. His tenaciousness would see to it.

At least four people hovered over him. They transferred him from the ambulance stretcher to the gurney by the blanket under him. The bright overhead lights burned through his closed eyelids. More voices. His oxygen was disconnected, and he struggled to breathe. Did they notice? Maybe. Maybe not. Before he went into full panic mode, he was connected to the ER's main lines.

A blood pressure cuff tightened on his arm then loosened. The rip of velcro followed the sensation as the band was removed. Something plastic squeezed his left middle finger.

Conversations, instructions, they were all a muffled noise. Despite not being able to focus on human interaction, his hearing and sense of smell were acute. Plastic packaging ripping open. The scents of bleach and hand sanitizer assailed his nostrils even though a mask covered his nose and mouth. Machines bleeped and pinged. Were they attached to him?

Why did he get involved with that dealer? The one with the reputation for cutting his drugs with whatever was at hand. At this moment, he hated himself. He deserved to die, not that he wanted to.

His awareness faded as he slipped into the abyss of death. The heart monitor stopped its intermittent pinging. The sound changed to a constant electronic monotone.

The flurry of activity surrounding him didn't change. Some other poor soul then? A different beeping floated over the din — a defibrillator. It grew faster, and the pings came closer together until they became one. A voice yelled 'clear.' He expected someone to put the paddles on his chest and shock him, but nothing happened.

More talk amongst the people surrounding him. A metal pole tipped over and landed with a crash. Shoes squeaked on the floor; the footsteps rapid. Someone running.

The emergency department at Vancouver General was a madhouse. Summer in the city brought out the worst in people, and summer hadn't officially arrived yet. It was only late May. Still almost a month before the solstice. Medical personnel ran from one spot to another, fetching equipment and supplies. Casualties waited, holding bloody bandages or ice packs on their wounds; their condition deemed not life-threatening so they could wait. Pity the poor triage staff on duty. Bleach overpowered the sour scent of vomit.

Well-thumbed magazines lie scattered on tables. Green paint; the colour a cross between mint and pea soup covered the walls; interspersed with patches of white where it had chipped off and left the plaster exposed.

A woman with an irritating nasal voice paged doctors and specialist surgeons. If Hilary had to listen to her all day, it would drive her bonkers.

In the corner, a mother tried to shush her screeching infant. The child's cries drew scowls from those seated in the waiting area. Luke glowered in the woman's direction.

"Give her a break; she's probably worn out. Poor little thing can't tell her mom what's wrong," said Hilary leaning against a wall near the reception area. In succession, she pressed her thumb on each finger of her right hand and cracked her knuckles.

"I am so glad mine are past that age. Listening to that for hours would do my head in."

"You're turning into an old curmudgeon. What's crawled up your butt tonight? You're not normally this crusty."

"Nothing," he said, raking his fingers through his shiny

black hair. "You know you're going to end up with arthritis if you keep doing that."

"Old wives' tale. Besides, it feels good."

The man was good-looking. No doubt about that, but he had a wife and two little girls; Leah, five and Emma, three. They had their father's black hair and dark brown eyes and the ability to wrap anyone around their pinky fingers. Luke's wife, Kim, was fair, pale-skinned, blonde-haired and blue-eyed. He obviously carried the dominant gene on the appearance front.

Something bothered him. He was in a mood before she spotted the overdose victim and his temperament deteriorated since.

Code blue blared over the loudspeakers, and everyone on staff raced to their positions. Two more crash carts were pushed through the doors to the treatment area, their wheels clattering on the tile floor. Did the OD victim go into cardiac arrest? He was alive when the paramedics bundled him into the ambulance.

A man of East-Indian extraction dressed in green scrubs, a surgical hat and bright yellow Crocs approached. "I'm Doctor Singh. I attended the patient you brought in." He removed a latex glove before reaching out to shake their hands.

"Was he the reason for calling the code?" asked Hilary.

"No. The patient is alive but still unconscious. It could be some time before he wakes; if he does. We've sent the syringe brought in by the paramedics to the lab for further tests on the contents. It's heroin, but there's an unknown substance mixed in. The EMTs said they administered Narcan but without result. We'll wait a bit and try again. The cutting agent could very well be what's causing him to remain comatose. They told us the syringe was still in his arm when you found him?"

"Yes. And blood had backed up into it. I don't like the sounds of this. A foreign substance. The heroin is bad enough."

"You'd think he'd have smelled something off but was likely so desperate for his fix; he didn't care."

"There have been several instances of bad drugs

circulating in the city of late." Hilary scribbled notes from her conversation with the doctor into her notepad.

Two

Hilary's house, East 7th Avenue, Vancouver

After a long shift, all Hilary wanted was to go home and soak in a hot bath. Today had been brutal, and the overdose victim and subsequent trip to the ER capped it — and not in a positive way.

Bulletproof vest removed and hung in her locker, her handcuffs, notepad and other things she didn't feel like dragging home well after midnight following. She unbuckled her holstered gun and dropped the sidearm and ammunition with the officer in charge of the secure weapon vault. Ready to leave, Hilary shrugged on her jacket and slung her crossbody purse strap over her shoulder.

Outside, Luke's mini-van tore out of the employee parking area. Something bothered him. It couldn't be job-related. He was a reputable cop. A clean cop. Not a bent one. It must be personal.

Hilary pushed the button on her key fob and pointed the device towards her bright red Kia Forte coupe. The lights flashed when the locks released. In minutes, she was behind the wheel and easing out of the parking lot. Her German Shepherd, Xena, would be desperate to get outside. She was a good dog.

Never had any accidents in the house, but the possibility existed when Hilary put in long days like this one.

One tired foot in front of the other, she trudged up the steps of her home on East 7th Avenue. The curtains twitched, and her dog's nose pressed against the glass. No sooner had the canine appeared in the front window, she disappeared. Hilary inserted the key in the lock, gave it a turn and pushed down on the handle.

A stack of mail lay on the floor, and she bent down to pick up the letters. She flipped through the assorted correspondence, as she walked through the house to let Xena out into the backyard. Advertising postcards for pizza, vinyl siding, stairlifts, and roofing, but amongst them was an official letter from the department.

Once she let the animal out, she ripped open the envelope. Her dog was in training to be a member of the Vancouver Police K-9 unit. Across the page in a bold red stamp was the word FAIL. The news crushed her. The pair were going to be partners. Hilary and Xena together twenty-four-seven.

A few minutes later, Xena scratched on the back door, and she let her in.

Something about finding the OD victim in the alley niggled at her. There was a familiarity to it, but why, when, or where eluded her. At least she had a few days off before returning to duty — time to get over Xena's failure at police dog training.

Hilary settled in on the sofa and turned on the television. Xena settled at her feet. Flipping through the channels looking for something to watch, reports of the overdose filled the screen on one of the local news networks. She sat the remote down beside her.

The reporter stood with her back to Vancouver General. The bright red emergency sign was visible over the woman's right shoulder. A strong wind whipped her blonde hair across her face, and she had to brush the windblown tresses away several times. In the months leading up to the present, overdoses had been on the rise. In fact, they were so frequent; they became barely newsworthy. Why this one? Had one of her colleagues or a member of the hospital staff spoken to the media?

Even though narcotics wasn't her department, fellow officers knew when a member of the drug squad was deep undercover. The overdose victim didn't look like anyone she had seen around police headquarters. If he were part of an official, covert operation that went wrong, then it would be news.

All the speculation over the identity of the victim and why he demanded media attention made Hilary's head ache. She turned the television off and went to the kitchen. Her dog followed along behind, so she let her outside again. While Xena explored the back yard, she reached into the cupboard for a glass, took her Brita jug out of the fridge and poured herself a cold drink.

Beverage in hand, she phoned the hospital. "Constable Dunbar, Badge 8652. My partner and I accompanied an ambulance bringing in an OD vic earlier tonight. I wondered if his condition has changed."

The line went dead momentarily, followed by elevator music. Thankfully, Hilary didn't have to listen to the racket for too long.

"ER," a female answered brusquely.

If the place was still crazy, she didn't blame the woman for being rude. The staff had been run off their feet earlier in the evening. Hilary repeated her query as well as identifying herself again.

"Nothing. Still unconscious. Waste of hospital resources," the woman said and hung up.

The last statement stunned Hilary. A scratch on the screen door snapped her from her reverie, and she let Xena back in and locked the house for the night.

When she started turning out lights and headed for the stairs, the pup bee-lined to follow and knocked her off balance scooting between her legs.

Three

When roll call ended, the duty sergeant pulled Hilary aside. "Message from the hospital. Your OD vic is awake. Contents of the syringe are known, too." He handed her a slip of paper.

Luke leaned against the doorframe with his arms folded across his chest. His posture spoke volumes about his mood.

"Thanks, Sarge," she said and strode across the room to where her partner stood. "Phone call to make before we head out. Go to the car, and I'll be right there."

"You're getting too involved in this overdose case. Leave it to the drug squad," Luke snapped.

Even though the other department specialized in that area, she found the victim. She was determined to keep going to the end, or at least until she had information to take to them to bring down the dealer.

Hilary stopped at her desk in the squad room and placed the call.

"Heroin was tainted. Guy is lucky to be alive. You don't shoot drain cleaner and warfarin into your veins and live to tell the tale. He's got horseshoes somewhere or an angel on his

13

shoulder."

"Does our vic have a name?"

Papers rustled. "Yes. Erik Layne. That's all we've managed to get out of him."

"Thanks. Hilary dropped into her chair. Drain cleaner and rat poison — the hallmark of Carlos Navarra, the most notorious dealer in Greater Vancouver. Her high school best friend, Taylor Simpson, got mixed up with this guy and died after injecting one of his noxious cocktails. Before that, the girls shared everything, including the same birthdate. Should she pass the case off to the proper team and walk away? Never.

Unpleasant memories from the time flooded back. Hilary blinked back tears. She couldn't lose control in the squad room. Deep breath taken, she strode out of the station and into the waiting cruiser.

"Well?" asked Luke drumming the steering wheel with his fingers.

"Heroin was cut with drain cleaner and rat poison."

"That's Carlos Navarra's trademark. You pass it on to the drug squad?"

"Not yet. Want to see if I can convince the vic to open up to me."

"You're crazy, woman." He turned the key, and they left the parking lot to begin their day.

By now, Erik's heroin withdrawal reached its peak. Alternating sweats and chills plagued him. Every part of his body ached, and his heart raced. The monitor read one hundred and fifty beats and still climbed. The vital organ would explode if it didn't slow down. Everything was blurred; his eyes watered so bad. He couldn't bend his head forward because his nose ran as if someone turned on a faucet in his head. Combined with these unpleasant symptoms, he was restless and had difficulty breathing. No matter how deeply he inhaled, it didn't seem like he was getting any air into his lungs.

Not until the vomiting and violent tremors started, did anything happen. Then, one of the staff members brought in a small plastic cup, the size the medical team used when dispensing meds, containing a red liquid.

"Drink this. It'll take the edge off."

His hand shook so bad, Erik couldn't hang on to it.

The attendant held it to his lips for him. "It's methadone. We'll start you at thirty-five milligrams and go from there. The dosage might have to be increased or decreased, but this is the recommended measure. The effects will kick in in a few minutes."

Erik sipped the medicine then flopped back on his bed. Relief couldn't come soon enough. "It's not working," he said.

"Give it a few minutes. You just swallowed the stuff. It takes time for your system to absorb the medication. I'll stick around until it starts to take effect."

Gradually, the methadone worked its magic. Erik's heart rate slowed, and he could breathe productively. The shaking brought on by the chills stopped, and his sinuses dried up.

"You're one lucky so-and-so. You could be a guest of our morgue rather than our ICU."

Lucky wasn't the word that came to Erik's mind. Not that he wanted to die, he just wanted the pain to go away.

"We should go to the hospital first. I want to talk to this Layne guy and the staff," said Hilary.

"I still say you should pass it over to the drug squad. Especially with Navarra being involved."

"I'll pass it to them when I'm good and ready."

Luke shook his head but drove to the hospital. They entered through the emergency department. The waiting area was as hectic as it was the night they brought in their OD victim. A harried nurse triaged patients and sent them to the chairs to wait for their turn. During a break between cases, the two walked to her station and stated their business.

The woman spun around in her chair and back. "He's busy with someone, but I'll have him come speak with you when he's free."

"Thanks," said Hilary.

A grunt escaped from Luke's lips.

Her partner was right. She was too involved, but he didn't know about her friend. It had become personal.

A short time later, Doctor Singh joined them. "Sorry to keep you waiting. The ER is a busy place."

"We're here to talk about the overdose patient we brought in a few nights ago."

"Ah, the young man." He fidgeted with the loose change in his pockets.

Even over the din, the coins clattering together were audible. "I heard it was tainted heroin," Hilary said.

"You heard correctly. Once we knew what we were dealing with, we gave the man a transfusion to rid his body of the contaminated blood."

"What can you tell us about him?"

Luke shot her a dirty look.

The physician plucked a file off the counter and flipped it open. He scanned the page. "Ah, here we go. Erik Layne. Early thirties. No fixed address. Been living rough and using hard drugs for as long as he can remember."

Hilary sighed. At least her friend, Taylor, had a home.

"Can we see him?"

"We've moved the young man to ICU."

"Thanks."

Luke grumbled the entire way to the room in the intensive care unit where Erik now resided. Hilary picked up the phone and stated their business at the entrance, and someone buzzed them through.

A nurse at the desk pointed to the room in question, and they walked in.

"How are you feeling?" asked Hilary.

"Wh-who are you?"

"We found you in Blood Alley and called for an ambulance. This is my partner, Luke Stephanopoulos. My name is Hilary. They tell me your name is Erik." She pulled a plastic chair towards the bed and sat.

Luke moved closer. He didn't trust this guy and seeing his fellow police officer in such proximity made his neck tingle.

"Can you tell us who you bought the heroin from?" she asked, pulling out her notebook.

Erik shook his head. His bloodshot eyes widened, pupils dilated wide, making the hazel irises practically invisible. What colour he had vanished, and he took on a ghostly pallor.

It was ninety-nine percent certain Carlos Navarra was behind it, but unlikely this guy would roll on him. Doing so would be an automatic death sentence.

"Did you know it was tainted? Drain cleaner and rat poison. You're lucky to be alive. We need you to help us rid the streets of this scumbag and into prison where he belongs."

"No. He'll kill me or have me killed if I say anything."

The rhythmic, yet monotone beeping of the machines sped up. The nurse who let them in earlier rushed across the hall and into the room. "I'm going to have to ask you both to leave. You're upsetting our patient."

"Come on, Hil. He's not going to give us squat. Turn it over to the drug squad like I said."

The monitors beeped faster than before. Erik's eyes widened in fright.

Hilary placed her hand on the back of his. "Sorry to upset you."

Outside the unit, she turned to her partner. "Did you see how scared he got when you mentioned turning it over to the drug squad? He was petrified."

"Ah, well, serves him right. Maybe a scare like that will do him good. Get him off the smack."

"I could smack you up the side of the head for saying that."

The two bickered all the way to the cruiser.

"I don't know what's gotten into you lately, but you're like a hungry bear waking from hibernation," she said, leaning on the roof of the car.

"Just stuff." He opened the driver's door and climbed in behind the wheel. Yes, Hilary would keep his confidence, but he was not prepared to share what might be nothing at all. He valued his privacy. Kim had been grumpy of late. Still, he assumed she was grieving the death of her grandmother and guilty because she couldn't go to her funeral in Northern Ontario. For now, things would remain as they were.

"Any time you want to talk. You know I'm here for you," Hilary said, easing into the passenger seat.

"Thanks."

The hospital quieted for the night. The corridor lights dimmed. All was quiet until a familiar gravelly voice whispered in his ear, "You're a dead man."

That sound. That smell. The man had terrible breath. Smelled like rotting flesh — the dealer's enforcer. How did he gain entry? Hospitalized frequently, and in this department, no one could enter without being let in. Did this guy let on he was a family member or a member of the drug squad?

If Erik were to leave ICU alive, instead of in a body bag, he had to escape and go into hiding. It was his only option. Waving his arms in the direction the sound and stench came from, it seemed the unwanted visitor had left the room. At least the unpleasant odour was no longer under his nostrils.

Erik tore the needles connected to his IV tubes out of his arms and pulled off the wires attached to his chest. Nurses descended on his room before he could go any further. He had set off the alarms.

"You can't do this," one exclaimed.

She was young. Barely out of nursing school, so however old that made her. Her scrub pants were bright orange. A Winnie the Pooh and Tigger print on her top. The girl's hair was the same colour as his sister's — ash blonde. Well, Serenity's hair used to be that shade. She could dye it now for all he knew.

"What are you trying to do?" the other healthcare provider asked.

This woman was probably in her mid to late forties, short and almost as big around as she was tall.

"Someone was here. Threatened me. I've got to leave. Not

safe here."

"Calm down," the older nurse soothed. "We'll get you settled and ensure you're safe."

"But ..."

The younger one, her name tag read Nancy, tried to lay him down, but he fought against her efforts. They didn't realize the severity of the situation. If he didn't get out of this place and Vancouver, he'd be hauled up in a fishing trawler's nets with their catch of the day.

Nancy stroked his hair. Her eyes widened in horror as she held up a shock about the diameter of a two-dollar coin in a gloved hand. His hair. She hadn't pulled. He didn't feel it become detached from his scalp. What happened?

The other healthcare provider, whose name he couldn't read because her tag had flipped around, pushed a button on the wall behind the head of his bed.

She removed her gloves and dropped them in the wastebasket before disappearing into the corridor.

When she returned, a hospital security guard accompanied her.

"A wannabe cop isn't going to be able to protect me. I need out. Now!"

"You're going nowhere until the doctor releases you. I've contacted the police, and there will be armed guards outside your room beginning tomorrow. In the meantime, you'll have to play nice and get along with Al."

Packages of saline, other liquids, and injection kits covered the surface of the tray table. Needles were inserted into his veins. Erik grimaced with each prick. Despite the fact he was a heroin addict, he hated the initial skin puncture and the burn of the drug entering his body.

Afterwards, the senior nurse hung the bags, connected the IV tubes, and attached the heart monitor leads to his chest and limbs.

After the nurse reconnected him to his drips and monitors, a pair of restraints were attached to the bed rails. The other end encircled his wrists. He yanked, trying to break the leather straps tying him to the bed, but no matter how hard he pulled, he could not free himself.

At roll call, the duty sergeant went over the priority cases. "We need a rotation of guards at Vancouver General. A patient is in danger." He rolled his eyes as he spoke. "Dunbar and Stephanopoulos, I believe this is your overdose victim from a few days ago."

"I'll go, Sarge. I don't mind," said Hilary. Anything to break free from Luke and his moods. Besides, while she sat in the hospital corridor, she could catch up on her reading. There would be precious little else to do.

Two other members of the force volunteered. The teams were shuffled to provide complete coverage, and everyone was dismissed.

"Thanks for bailing on me," said Luke.

His voice was snarky. Rightfully so. By Hilary taking the first rotation in the protection detail, it lumbered him with Rodriguez. A rookie. Oh well. Maybe by the time the security detail finished, Luke would be reasonably human. Or at least back to his usual crusty self.

Hilary signed out a car and drove through the busy streets to the hospital. Once there, she parked in one of the many slots allotted for the constabulary. Between traffic accidents, drug overdoses, and other incidents, there was almost always at least one of their vehicles there.

After stopping at admitting to inquire if he was still a patient in intensive care, Hilary traversed the corridors to the unit. The nurse at the desk buzzed her in. A security guard stood as she approached.

"You're my replacement then," he said, stretching as he spoke. "Was quiet most of the night. No one came or went other than the nurses on midnights."

"Thanks."

Copy of *Hello* magazine retrieved from her handbag, she shoved the purse on the floor under her seat. The plastic chair was hard and uncomfortable. She leafed through the pages, not absorbing the photographs or the text.

Head tipped back against the glass wall, Hilary sighed. If she were to continue this assignment for much longer, a more comfortable chair was required. Yes, she volunteered for the post, but a creature comfort or two wouldn't go amiss.

Standing, Hilary stretched. She laced her fingers together above her head, cracked her knuckles, then bent over and let her arms fall limp. Movement repeated a few times, the kinks and aches dissipated.

A nurse exited the room. "You okay, hon?"

"Yeah. Just stiff."

"Softer chair in there." She hooked her thumb in the direction of the patient's accommodations.

"Thanks. I'll take you up on that." Belongings gathered up, she walked into the room and deposited them on the window sill. Afterwards, she sank into the padded armchair — an addition from when she first visited Erik in this room.

"Urnghmmm …," he groaned and smacked his lips. The mattress and bedsprings creaked as he shifted position.

"Sorry. Didn't mean to wake you," said Hilary walking towards his bed. Her police boots clomped on the floor with each step. "What are these doing?" she pointed to his hands. "Excuse me; I'll be right back. Someone has some explaining to do."

She stormed out of the room to the nurses' station. "Why on earth do you have that man in restraints?"

"He pulled his IV tubes out and was trying to leave," said the young woman wearing a Winnie the Pooh and Tigger print top. Her name tag read Nancy.

"They come off now. Do I make myself clear? No one on my watch is going to be shackled to their bed."

"But …"

Hilary didn't wait for an answer. She strode back to Erik's room.

At his bedside, Hilary unbuckled the leather straps. "How's that?"

"Better." Erik rubbed his wrists and turned his head

towards her.

Hair remained on his pillow: not just a few strands but great clumps leaving toonie-sized bald spots on his scalp. Hilary attempted to mask the look of shock on her face.

"Hair, right? The first time it happened, the nurse looked like that, but she held it in her hand." He chuckled. "Guess I'll have to start shaving my head."

She smiled, happy to see he had a sense of humour in spite of everything.

Her jet-black hair, parted down the centre, was pulled back in a bun at the nape of her neck. Her ebony eyes sparkled when she smiled, revealing straight white teeth. If she wore makeup, it was very little. What would she look like with her hair down? How long was it?

Many of the women he'd seen while living on the streets were hardened and aged beyond their years. But living and sleeping rough, mixed with drugs, did that. He suspected his appearance was similar. With his hair falling out in chunks because of the stuff he shot into his veins and poor diet, how could it not be?

This woman was different; fresh-faced, young and attractive. What was her name? She introduced herself and her partner when he first emerged from the coma, but for the life of him, he could not remember. If he asked her name, would she think he was hitting on her? He swallowed hard. "Sorry, I know you introduced yourself, but for the life of me, I can't remember what you said your name was. I feel like an idiot having to ask."

"Hilary."

"That's right. Now I remember." Erik shifted in his bed, trying to find a comfortable position and maintain his modesty. Hospital issue, split-back nightgowns did nothing to help in that regard. At least now, the restraints were gone.

Four

Police Headquarters, Cambie Street, Vancouver

After spending her shift at the hospital, Hilary returned to the police station. Once through the security door, the duty officer handed her a note. She scanned it, mumbled a thank you, and hurried to a room where Sergeant Vincent and two members of the drug squad waited.

"Nice of you to join us," an Oriental man dressed in a blue-grey suit said. "Sun Huang." He introduced himself before standing and reaching out to shake her hand. His tie hung loosely at the neck and the top button of his shirt was undone. He pushed his black, plastic rimmed glasses up his nose as he spoke. "My colleague here is Robert MacDonald."

"The message said there is surveillance footage from the security cameras."

"You can call me Bob." The other specialty policeman nodded and pushed a button on the remote.

Judging by his unkempt appearance, the man must be on an undercover assignment. His plainclothes were grubby; his hair long and stringy. What might have posed at one time as a neatly trimmed beard on his long, thin face was bushy and overgrown.

The wide-screen TV flickered to life. Albeit somewhat grainy, the picture quality was decent enough to identify people and objects. Erik's huddled form next to one of the dumpsters came into focus. With eyes fixed on the video, Hilary chewed on her bottom lip, waiting for the deal to go down. The pop of cracking knuckles drew dirty looks from her colleagues.

"We've seen this already," her superior said and nodded to the keeper of the remote. He pushed another button and the images on the screen fast-forwarded to a couple of hours later. A figure wearing a hoodie approached. Head down; it was impossible to determine the person's identity. The suspect stopped at Erik's feet and kicked at them. The deal went down, and the mystery person turned and walked away from the camera, and the screen went black.

"You didn't get anything else?" Hilary asked.

"Not from that camera." The man pressed the play button once more.

This time the camera was mounted on the same side of the alley as Erik. Hilary sucked in a deep breath and chewed her bottom lip, hoping this would be the footage needed to bring Carlos Navarra down and lock him away for many years.

The video began. Again, they watched the figure in the hoodie approach, head down shielding his face. Thanks to the camera's location when he passed the package to their victim, Hilary spotted it. "Stop. I saw something on the back of his hand."

It took a bit of fiddling, reversing and forwarding one frame at a time to reach the correct one. When on it, Hilary said, "Can you blow that up?"

Gradually, the image of a giant spider on a syringe came into focus. "That's Navarra himself. I'd recognize that tattoo anywhere."

"We'll have this printed and circulated to the rest of the drug squad. With any luck, Mr. Navarra will be spending tonight and the rest of his natural behind bars as a guest of Her Majesty," the stockier of the two detectives said. With the dealer's ID confirmed, they leapt to their feet and dashed out of the room.

The sergeant folded his arms over his chest and leaned back in his seat. Hilary slumped back in her chair. A reprimand was coming, or worse. Disciplinary action even. Why didn't she listen to Luke and hand the case to the drug squad straight away?

"Well, Dunbar, can you enlighten me?"

"Sir. I-I should have gone to the drug squad, but I couldn't. Not until I was sure. Once we found out what the heroin was cut with, I knew."

"And will your victim testify in court?"

"I doubt it. He's terrified of Navarra, which is why he wanted the police guard at the hospital."

"Up to you to persuade him. From what I've been hearing, you have a relationship of sorts with him."

Hilary stood and walked towards the door. About halfway across the room, she stopped and turned around. "I wouldn't call it that, but I'll try to convince him to make a statement or something to help put Navarra away for good." She paused, then continued. "There's something else. I haven't told anyone about it before."

He leaned forward and placed his elbows on the desk's surface and folded his hands.

"One of my best friends." She choked back a sob.

"Take your time."

A memory from a happier time when the girls were teens flooded back. They went hiking at the Whistler Train Wreck. On the suspension bridge spanning the rushing Cheakamus River, Taylor started jumping up and down, making the walkway undulate. Hilary had grabbed the handrail and begged her friend to stop, but her pleas only brought laughter. Taylor bounded off the bridge laughing, while Hilary stayed put, clinging to the railing until the bridge quit swaying so she could move to safety. It was a bittersweet trip. Not long after they came home, Taylor started taking drugs.

"She got mixed up with Navarra and died after shooting up one of his noxious concoctions. It was after that; I decided to become a cop." Her tears flowed freely now. The image of Taylor's body laid out in the casket at her funeral with her mother and father clinging to one another. Their bodies wracked with sobs fresh in her memory.

"Pull yourself together," the sergeant said. He removed a handkerchief from his trouser pocket and passed it to her before standing and walking to the door. "Take as much time as you need. I'll make sure you're not disturbed."

She nodded and turned away. No matter how much she wanted to breathe a sigh of relief over the lack of disciplinary action, she was too upset. Never, in all her years on the force, had she broken down and cried in front of anyone. If she cried, she did it in the privacy of her home. Until today, that is.

That evening as Hilary was preparing to leave, the two detectives from the drug squad brought an uncooperative, struggling Carlos Navarra into the station. With his hands cuffed behind his back, the man jerked one way, then the other trying to escape their clutches. Rather than leave, she followed them towards the interview room. "Mind if I sit in?"

The suspect shot her a venomous look. If it was an intimidation tactic, it didn't work.

Sun Huang hooked his thumb in the direction of the adjacent room. Hilary waited for them to enter the interrogation room, then walked into the smaller one. Behind the two-way mirror, she had an unobstructed view of the questioning. She pushed a button activating the speaker.

Huang retreated to the corner. Bob pushed the suspect into the chair on the far side of the table and took a position facing him.

Hilary had spent time in the interview rooms before, but never for anything this vital. A video camera mounted near the ceiling in the opposite corner focused on the interviewee.

The first photo, complete with time and date stamp, was placed on the table in front of the handcuffed prisoner. "What can you tell us about this, Navarra?" Bob MacDonald demanded.

No answer.

"We can take all night. No skin off our noses. Take

another look." The cop pushed the picture closer to him.

Carlos smirked. "Not anything to do with me," he sneered, showing off a gold incisor.

"Really. How about this one?" The officer placed the picture taken from the second surveillance camera in front of him. "Or this?" The close-up of the man's hand with the identical tattoo was flopped down on top of the others.

"It's you, isn't it?" Sun said, leaning into the man's face.

"So?" He tried to stand, but the well-dressed detective pushed him back into the chrome-legged, plastic chair.

"And he's the addict who's still in the hospital thanks to your smack." The image on the top of the stack was moved aside, and a stubby finger stabbed at the overdose victim.

Navarra's smirk faded.

"Would you show our guest to one of our finest cells, Bob?" The sarcasm in Sun's voice came through loud and clear.

MacDonald hauled Carlos to his feet and escorted him out the door.

Hilary met them in the corridor. "Now what?" she asked.

"We've got him on trafficking charges for now. Waiting for a warrant to search his premises. No doubt we'll find more drugs there. Then we'll have him on possession with intent as well."

Five

Vancouver General Hospital, West 12th Avenue, Vancouver

Hilary waited until the following day to tell Erik what went down since the last time she visited. In the meantime, the order had been issued, and Navarra's home searched.

"Good news. Navarra is behind bars, and he'll be spending quite a bit of time in a seven-square metre cell. Trafficking, possession with intent, weapons. They got quite the haul when they executed the search warrant."

Erik's face paled. "What happens to me when I get released? One of Navarra's heavies will come looking for me. I'm done. You interfering police have signed my death warrant." He paced in his room, flexing his fingers as he walked.

"I think you're exaggerating. Navarra's thugs won't come near you. By that time, his entire gang will be locked up."

Fingers laced together he placed his palms on top of his head and turned to face her. His voice shook as he spoke. "You don't know that. You have no clue how wide a network the man has. The ones you don't arrest will move in and take over

— including paybacks. I'm so far in debt to him; I'll never escape. That's why I got the tainted smack. Rid himself of me for good or scare me bad enough, I'll do anything to get the money I owe him."

Hilary placed her hand on his left forearm, and he recoiled at her touch.

"You can bet they're saying it was me who stitched him up," he said, sweeping his arms down to his sides. Erik backed towards the corner and slid down the wall. Once on the floor, he drew his knees towards his chest and wrapped his arms around them. Head bowed, he made himself as small as possible, given his stature.

She joined him on the floor. With her legs straight in front of her, she crossed one foot over the other. After his reaction the last time she touched him, she didn't dare. At least not so soon. "I viewed Navarra's interview with Huang and MacDonald from the drug squad. I doubt the scumbag will come looking for you. I was the one that recognized the tattoo on the back of his hand from the Blood Alley security camera footage."

He lifted his head and looked at her through terror-stricken eyes. His face was ghostly white, and his lips were dry and cracked. "B-but, he'll still think I told you."

Erik's life could be in danger because of the arrest. How could she protect him from Navarra's thugs? The force couldn't dedicate around-the-clock protection for him forever. Staff Sergeant Wilde was complaining about the resources being tied up. Hilary overheard a heated conversation between the woman and Sergeant Vincent before she left the station. The senior officer threatened to take it to the top if need be.

Erik's methadone treatment progressed slowly. The correct dosage still hadn't been discovered, so before the allotted time was up, his withdrawal symptoms returned. While not as severe as before, they remained unpleasant. The chills, shakes, and sweats were terrible enough, but the stomach cramps and subsequent diarrhea wore him down.

As tempted as he was to return to the streets and his old habits, the hospital was warm and dry, had a comfortable bed and regular meals. The unpleasantness was tolerable, yet he hoped they would soon find the right amount to give him.

That night, a different nurse brought his small measure of methadone. He slurped it down — at least it tasted decent — and handed her back the empty medication cup. Within seconds of her leaving, the heroin entered his system. His vision blurred. His tongue numbed. His coordination was off, and he was unable to find the call button. Had someone moved it to prevent him from calling for help? He tried to shout but couldn't find his voice. The only thing he could do was knock down his IV pole.

The metal on tile crash brought the staff to his room. Erik drifted in and out of consciousness.

"He's high on heroin," one said.

"How?" another inquired.

"In his methadone?"

"Who brought it to him?"

"Let's save that for later. The patient needs a dose of Naloxone."

Rubber soles on shoes squeaked on the floor as someone raced out of his room. The IV tube tugged when one of the medical staff righted the pole. Soon after, the anti-opiate fluid entered his arm through a port on the needle. The symptoms eased, and he came around.

"Someone tampered with my methadone," Erik hollered.

"Impossible. Are you sure someone didn't smuggle you in some heroin?" asked the oldest of the medical staff in attendance.

"No," he spat. "Someone has already snuck in and threatened me. It had to be him." Panic coursed through him. First, a threat and now an unknown person tampered with his methadone.

Navarra meant business. The man was crazy and didn't care who he hurt. Anyone deemed a threat to his empire; he employed one of his loyal gang members to eliminate the risk — real or perceived.

One of the nurses called through to security. Al, who had been assigned to stand guard after Erik's visit from his unwelcome guest with halitosis, soon appeared in the doorway. Cameras were installed in ICU as a precaution but more for the nurses to monitor the patients and be ready to act if one took a turn.

"By now, the recordings from the night I spent here on watch would be recorded over. I'm sure of that," Al said. "Shall I call in the police?"

"Yes," Erik demanded.

An hour later, staff buzzed two plainclothes detectives into the unit. Erik's room was across from the nurses' station, so he had a front-row seat to the activity. One of the men was Oriental and shorter and stalkier than the other, who was quite tall and slim. They introduced themselves as Huang and MacDonald. Between the room's glass wall and the open door, he saw and heard most everything.

The taller detective entered Erik's room wearing blue latex gloves. He rifled through the garbage can, looked under the bed, nightstand and the cabinet housing a small stainless-steel sink.

"You looking for the medicine cup that my methadone was in? You won't find it here. I gave it back to the nurse when I finished with it."

The detective scowled at him and left without saying a word.

Since coming out of the coma, Erik had several nurses. How did he establish she wasn't a member of the hospital staff? Better yet, how did she gain access? The cops had to be let in. Intensive Care is supposed to be a secure unit, isn't it?

ICU nurses and police turned intensive care over searching for the small plastic cup.

"I found it," the head nurse yelled from her hands and knees.

"Don't touch it," barked one of the officers.

She stood, brushed off the knees of her pants and moved

aside.

By now, the nurse who brought Erik his maintenance treatment had long since disappeared. The ICU staff and police huddled around the desk with the detectives watching the monitors.

The mysterious woman appeared on the screen. Head down to protect her identity, she entered Erik's room, administered his methadone, and scurried away.

"She's not one of us," the head nurse stated with conviction. "I know all my girls, and she's not one of mine."

"Could she be from a different unit? Shift?" asked MacDonald.

"No."

"Someone pretending to be a member of the hospital staff on the loose in Vancouver General Hospital, that does not bode well," said Huang pulling out his cell phone.

The detective never raised the phone to his ear, so he either sent a text or an email.

Erik likened the activity to an episode of a police procedural on the television, except it was *his* life in danger. He watched plenty of them over the years. Many from outside appliance stores that left the TVs in their windows turned on twenty-four hours a day. The sounds from the corridor softened. Now, he didn't hear much of what was said, if anything.

Before the end of their shift, the suspicious vessel and its contents would be in the police lab for analyzing.

Erik didn't need to receive the results of the analysis. They would come back as pure, uncut heroin.

The head nurse entered his room and disconnected the monitors from him and the wall. "You're well enough to be in a regular ward now. We're moving you to Mental Health and Substance Use. Whoever was behind the attack will think you died, and you'll be safe there."

"No. You can't!"

"The police are keeping the fact you survived quiet for your own protection."

"She's right," said MacDonald as he strolled through the doorway. "Besides, it gives us more time to find the perp."

"It's Carlos Navarra behind it. I'll stake my life on it." Erik's voice raised with each word.

The detective raked his fingers through his hair. "Can't be him. He's residing in one of our cells."

"One of his thugs then. Think he can't get word to his people on the outside? If you do, then you're dumber than you look."

"We've dealt with this scumbag before and ones like him."

"I have, too. I know what I'm talking about." Erik gripped the sheets and squeezed, his temper rising.

"You, out. I won't have you disturbing my patient," said the head nurse pointing the door to the cop. "And you, lay back and relax."

Heart racing, Erik did as the woman ordered. No one knew the danger he was in, and he was unable to convey it to anyone.

Before the end of the night, the ICU staff under the watchful eye of Al moved Erik to the secure unit.

Six

Vine Street, Vancouver

Two months later ...

It rained overnight, and now in the sweltering heat of the early morning, the sidewalks dried, sending steam into the air as the temperatures soared. The uniforms were hot enough, but the bulletproof vest made the sultry conditions unbearable.

With any luck, once the moisture from the asphalt and cement boiled off, the humidity level would drop, making the temperature tolerable. Thankfully, the police car had air conditioning, so the sticky unpleasantness outside their four doors was irrelevant until they had to attend a call.

About an hour or so into their day, the call blared out from the radio.

"All available units. Domestic violence reported at 99 Vine Street. Suspect is armed and dangerous. Woman held hostage at the location."

"Great. Of all the shouts, these are the worst. You never know what will happen," said Luke.

"Fingers crossed, another team has this resolved, and the creep cuffed by the time we get there."

Roof lights and siren activated, he steered the Charger through traffic, weaving around slower vehicles and speeding through intersections.

Just their luck, they arrived first on the scene. So much for things being wrapped up when they pulled up near the house.

Hilary broke protocol by not waiting for the SWAT team to secure the scene before jumping into action. Weapon drawn, she worked her way to the back of the one-and-a-half-storey clapboard house, keeping close to the structure. Sweat dripped down the back of her neck, soaking her collar. She wiped her forehead with her sleeve to prevent the moisture from dripping into her eyes, keeping arms extended, and her finger on the trigger of the handgun.

Inside, a woman screamed. Not taking her safety into account, Hilary stepped into the open ready to fire. Pop! The noise was innocuous enough. It reminded her of the cap guns she and her brothers played with as children. Pain seared through her lower left leg. Unable to support her weight, she collapsed. Hit. As she fell, her finger squeezed the trigger, and she fired her gun.

Why was she so stupid? Did she cause the hostage harm with her reckless actions? She hoped not. Now the job she coveted was gone. She'd be lucky if they didn't fire her after this. God, she was stupid. Not only that, but she disgraced her family, especially those who went before her in law enforcement. A tear ran down her face towards her ear. She was powerless to dash it away.

"Officer down. Officer down," Luke shouted into his handset. He needed to remove Hilary from harm's way before the perpetrator fired more shots.

Crouching as he ran, he darted to her side. Blood gushed from a hole in the left leg of her trousers. Stupid, useless vests did nothing for wounds below the waist. He grabbed her arms and dragged her behind a tree.

"Stay with me, partner. You're not dying on this watch."

Her skin grew pale and clammy to the touch. "Xena. Promise me you'll look after her. She's home alone. Take her to your house. The girls will love having her there."

The woman had a point. She wouldn't be able to care for a dog while she was laid up in the hospital. Yes, his daughters would love having a pet, even temporarily. His wife? Not so much.

The wail of a siren grew louder then stopped. Luke lifted his head. The ambulance approached from the street that butted to the one where they waited. No lights. No sound. Another vehicle followed. Big and black. One of theirs. The SWAT team. Why didn't they turn up sooner? Secure the scene. Had they, Hilary wouldn't have been shot.

An unmarked cruiser pulled up, and two plainclothes exited and took refuge on the far side of their vehicle. Drug squad. Huang and MacDonald. Why them? Were they in the area and stopped to offer assistance? Or, was whoever shot Hilary a person of interest in one of their cases? Could it? No.

The paramedics exited their emergency vehicle. The stretcher piled with medical equipment was unloaded and moved to the sidewalk. Until the scene was secured, they wouldn't come close.

Sharpshooters circled the home, high-powered rifles at the ready. One member pressed himself against the back wall of the house next to the door and broke the window before lobbing a tear gas canister through the hole.

Once the situation was deemed safe with the perpetrator incapacitated, the SWAT team rushed the building.

Now, the EMTs ran towards Luke and Hilary's location and went to work on her. They cut through the hem of her pant leg then ripped it the rest of the way to her groin. The gunshot wound, bleeding profusely, tore away much of the flesh and bone fragments showed through the darkened mess.

Bile rose in Luke's throat, and he turned away and vomited. Even in her weakened condition, he didn't want his partner to witness him distressed.

In her semi-conscious state, she mumbled his name. He

knelt near her head, mindful of staying out of the paramedics' way. "The EMTs are here. They'll look after you."

"Please, please take care of my dog," she whispered before losing consciousness.

"Get her on the gurney. We don't have time to stabilize her here. She needs to go to the hospital and now," one yelled.

As they bundled Hilary into the ambulance, Luke grabbed the keyring off her belt. On it was the key to her locker where she kept her purse and house keys. He watched the ambulance disappear, then schlepped to the cruiser and slumped in the driver's seat. How much time had elapsed since the call came in? Since he put out the 'officer down' shout?

He scrubbed his hands down his face. Kim needed to know. She would automatically think the worst if she heard the news on the radio or TV. Luke pulled his BlackBerry Z10 out of the holster to place the call. It vibrated. Startled, he let go like his hand had been scorched, and the phone fell to the floor. He fished around between the pedals and his size twelves until he found it. His wife's cell number showed on the screen. He pressed re-dial.

"Lukas, what's going on? Are you okay? Were you there?"

"I'm fine. Yes, we were on the shout. My partner, you know Hilary, somebody shot her."

"Is she …?"

"Don't know. The EMTs just took her away in the ambulance. I've got to go. I'll see you later." Luke ended the call. He didn't need the added aggravation. The endless nagging. Why had he joined the force? She didn't want to be a cop's wife, much less a widow. Kim's voice echoed in his head.

There would be reams of paperwork to fill out. Interviews. Internal affairs would stick their mitts into it. In addition to breaking protocol, Hilary fired her weapon. Luke turned the key, and the engine roared to life. Transmission in gear, he drove to the hospital for word on his partner's condition.

Luke eased the cruiser into the last police parking bay.

He wiped his palms on his thighs before climbing out and heading towards the emergency entrance. The automatic doors swished open as he approached. More uniforms than civilians filled the waiting area. "Any word yet?" he asked.

"Took her straight to surgery."

"Someone asked about next-of-kin," another co-worker said.

Things had gone from bad to worst. A strong possibility loomed that she wouldn't make it. "Should be in her personnel file at the station."

How could he cope, not knowing Hilary's condition? The two had been partners for three years. Always had the other's backs in dangerous situations. Knew their reactions. At first, he had been reluctant to be partnered with a woman, but now, he wouldn't have it any other way. She was a good cop. A smart cop. Why did she act recklessly at the scene? Not wait for the SWAT team. Step out into the open. Did she see or hear something inside the house?

The hours ticked by. Still no word on Hilary's condition. Shouldn't someone come out and give them a progress report? Luke stood and paced in one of the aisles rubbing the back of his neck as he walked. He should go back to headquarters, pick up her house keys and get her dog and all its accoutrements.

As he was about to leave, a surgeon came into the room. Blood covered his scrubs and his bright orange rubber boots. Every member of the force in the place stood. "Well?" asked Luke.

The man pulled off his surgical cap, mopped his forehead with it, then spoke. "We did everything we could, but …"

"She's dead?"

"Heavens no. Her leg was badly damaged. So much so, that no matter how hard we tried, we couldn't save it. The harder we worked, the more her condition deteriorated. In the end, we had to amputate below the knee."

Seven

Police Headquarters, Cambie Street, Vancouver

The questions started the moment Luke stepped through the main door of police headquarters. His head swam, trying to comprehend what was said and by whom. All he wanted was to go to Hilary's locker, retrieve her house keys, purse, and any other personal effects and leave.

In the locker room, he dropped to the bench between the rows of steel cabinets. This was the first time since he joined the force someone this close to him had suffered such a severe injury. The situation hit him like a punch in the stomach. Luke buried his head in his hands.

Soon after, the seat lurched, and a hand touched his back. "Sorry to hear about Dunbar. She's a good cop. We'll miss her."

Luke stared at him and nodded. "Thanks, Sarge. Only here to pick up her keys so I can collect her dog. Kids will love having a pet. Not so sure about the wife."

"You'll do what you have to do. I'll leave you to it. If you need anything, say the word."

"Will do."

"By the way, Huang and MacDonald arrested the shooter."

He cocked his head to the side. "Huh?" Why would the drug squad arrest a domestic violence perp?

"Seems the guy has been under our narcs' radar for some time. He was part of Navarra's organization. His number one thug."

That drug addict they stopped to help at Hilary's insistence in Blood Alley that night. They should never have gotten involved. She had to do the right thing and rescue the guy. On top of that, she volunteered to guard his room for pity's sake. What did her nobility get her? Shot.

The more those thoughts rattled around in his mind, the angrier he got. Next time he saw that addict, he'd let him have it.

"Look after yourself, Stephanopoulos. Don't need you out of circulation, too."

Did the man read his thoughts? After the Sergeant left, Luke inhaled deeply, stood and retrieved the property from Hilary's locker.

Shortly after nine o'clock, Luke pulled the family minivan to a stop outside Hilary's townhouse on East 7th Avenue. He clambered out from behind the wheel and started for the front door. As he lifted his foot to climb the steps, it hit him. She wouldn't be able to enter her own house. No way she could navigate stairs with only one leg. He managed to reach the top step before slumping to the verandah, where he buried his head in his arms, laced his fingers behind his head, and wept. The enormity of the day now sinking in.

How long he remained there, he didn't know. With no more tears to cry for his partner, he stood and let himself into the house. "Hi, Xena," he said to the barking dog. "Hilary isn't coming home for a while, so she asked me to come for you and your things. You'll be staying with my family for a while. I have two little girls who will love you." Egads! He had lost his mind. Talking to a dog like another person. Desperate times and all.

Xena quieted, and he started to collect her things and put

them by the front door. If everything were in one place, the van would be easier to load. Kim wouldn't be impressed. Leah and Emma would be ecstatic having a dog for the foreseeable.

About to take the first load out, he spotted a sheet of paper on the otherwise spotless living room floor. The intention was only to place the letter on the coffee table. The official logo on the letterhead beckoned him to examine it more closely. Xena failed canine training with the Vancouver Police. Was that part of Hilary's motive for taking a chance with her life earlier?

With the letter tucked into his pocket, Luke took the dog's paraphernalia to the van. When he returned, he put her collar around her neck and clipped the leash to it. House locked and key pocketed, the two descended the steps. He gave Xena a chance to sniff about the lawn and do her business before bundling her into the van.

The entire drive home, he worried about his wife's reaction to their temporary, four-legged, hair-shedding houseguest. So much so, after he pulled into the shared driveway on East 22nd Avenue, he remained in the vehicle mustering up the courage to go into the house. Pathetic. A cop who is afraid of his wife. He sucked in a deep breath, grabbed Xena's leash and the pair walked to the house.

Compared to Hilary's place, his two-bedroom home was a dive. Dark blue wooden shingle siding, many pieces of which had long since fallen off. The roof needed replacing. At least the front didn't appear too rundown. Indoors, the hardwood floors in the living room and small office/craft space had been sanded and stained.

The two bedrooms and the hall between needed to be refinished, but that wouldn't happen until next year. Same with the kitchen floor. At least there was a door in between the two rooms they could keep closed, and did. The sunroom off the back of the house would make the ideal place to store Xena's food.

His wife did a fantastic job decorating the small home. What she couldn't find in a thrift shop or at a flea market, she made. The woman had a knack for coordinating different shades and textures. The small room off the living room housed her cabinet style sewing machine and bins of fabric.

After letting himself in, he kept the dog on her lead. He didn't need her running riot straight off. At least give her a minute or two to sniff out the change in accommodations then set her free.

"Daddy, you got us a dog," Leah squealed.

Kim rounded the corner, wiping her hands with a tea towel. "What is … that," she asked when he extended his arms to hug her.

"That, as you so eloquently phrased it, is Hilary's dog. She made me promise to bring her home with me and take care of her before they took her away."

"Just how long is this, this hairball going to be stuck with us?"

"However long it takes. The doctors ended up amputating Hilary's leg."

Emma appeared, and she and her older sister fell to their knees in front of Xena. Hugs, cuddles and doggie kisses took over the moment, replacing the tension between him and his wife and the results of his partner's surgery.

"What are you still doing up?"

"Mom said we could stay up until you got home. Said you needed hugs from us."

"I sure do." Luke squatted and wrapped his arms around his daughters.

"I-I'm sorry. I didn't know. Are you okay?" Kim interrupted the father-daughter moment.

"No. I'm not okay. Not by any stretch." He turned to the girls. "You two, it's bedtime. I'll be there to tuck you in soon. Your mom and I need to talk."

Kisses administered to the tops of their heads; the girls scampered off, leaving Luke in an awkward situation with his wife.

"We need to talk, Lukas. I mean it," said Kim.

"Let me go say goodnight to the girls and get them settled first," he said then left the room. "Come on, Xena. You can spend the night with Leah and Emma." He picked up the sherpa bed and tucked it under one arm and headed to the girls' bedroom at the back of the house next to the kitchen.

In the short time the dog had been in the house; hair littered the hardwood floor. The home wasn't new, but on their salaries at the time of purchase, it was the best they could do. Their two daughters needed rooms of their own.

Kim started for the closet in the office/craft space to get the electric broom to clean up the dog hair, but Luke returned before she had the chance. He took her hand and led her to the couch. His olive skin, shiny black hair and chiselled features reminded her why she fell in love with him.

In the beginning, she didn't mind being a policeman's wife. Things were quiet, and he was safe. Lately, there were so many incidents and close calls, and she hated it. Gangs and drug use, and today, he could have been the one shot. She sat down beside her husband but immediately stood again. With her back to him, she chewed on her lower lip. "I can't do this anymore," she eventually said.

"Can't do what?"

"Be married to a cop." She turned around. Tears burned her eyes and blurred her vision.

"What are you saying?" Luke jumped up and pulled her into his arms.

She pushed herself free. "Today, it could have been you. Until I heard your voice, I thought the worst. Thought I would be a widow raising two little girls on my own, and it's not just what happened today."

"Today scared me, too. Thankfully, domestics this violent don't happen regularly."

"But what about the gangs, the dealers, dirty needles?"

"We wear protection for a reason."

"And look what good it did your partner. She got shot in the leg."

"A fluke."

"Try telling her that," she said, her voice shaking. "I want a divorce." Kim fled from the room.

Luke chased after her. The scene in the kitchen broke his heart. Kim stood with her back to him, braced against the counter, her body convulsing with sobs. Her revelation gutted him. She and the girls were his life. He couldn't lose them.

He strode across the room and paused about a foot away from her. Did he reach out and take her in his arms? Let her be? In her current state, she wouldn't thank him for either. In the end, he placed his hands on her upper arms but didn't try to turn her around to face him. Luke inched his way closer to her until their bodies touched. He moved her hair away from her neck and placed a soft kiss on the exposed skin before wrapping his arms around her waist.

Her hands found the backs of his and her palms rested against them. Her body shuddered against his when she drew in a ragged breath.

"I don't want to lose you," he whispered in her ear.

"I can't go on not knowing, if you're safe, or if you're hurt, or if you're lying someplace dead."

"I love my job. I can't just quit."

"If the girls and I mean anything to you, you will." She pushed her way out of his embrace and dashed to their bedroom, slamming the door behind her.

"Daddy, what was that?" asked Leah.

"I'm scared," said Emma.

He wanted to talk some sense, or at least try, into his wife, but his girls were his current priority. He turned on their bedroom light and sat down on his oldest daughter's bed. Emma scrambled out of hers and up beside him.

"Mommy is worried. My patrol partner got hurt today at work, and she's afraid it will happen to me," he explained without going into detail.

Leah tossed the covers aside and clambered to his side, not already occupied by her sibling.

Xena joined in the fracas and barked.

"Shh," he ordered, but his command was ignored. The puppy continued bouncing with the girls and barking. He tried again but to no avail. Finally, he plucked the canine off the bed and returned her to her own. "Stay," he said and pointed his index finger at her.

No wonder the dog failed police training. Mind of its own, for sure.

Eight

Vancouver General Hospital, West 12th Avenue,
Vancouver

Boredom set in. No glass walls overlooking a desk and the comings and goings of staff and visitors. Lounges with comfortable furniture and flatscreen TVs mounted on the walls occupied space at either end of the unit.

There was only so much daytime television Erik could tolerate. Being in the Mental Health and Substance Use ward didn't help matters. He got about twelve hours out of a dose of methadone, so when he received it first thing in the morning, he was fine until early evening. Some of the patients were far worse off than he, so at least he was thankful for that.

Until someone tampered with his medication, his recovery from heroin addiction, in his eyes, had progressed well. It was only a crutch that got him off one drug and on to another, but this one kept the demons of heroin withdrawal away. Well, if he received it on time.

Since his admission into this wing, he spent much time walking up and down the halls. There was only one way in with steel fire doors with panic bars installed in them. A camera aimed towards them monitored the comings and goings of everyone. Swipe-card door lock readers mounted on the walls ensured the security of the unit. Every inch of the public section was familiar to him.

He wandered down the corridor glancing in as he passed other patients' rooms. Depending on which side of the room the door was located, he caught glimpses of the occupants. Rumour had it, a well-known athlete was on this floor, but in all Erik's wanderings, he never encountered the man.

A window at the end of the corridor looked out over another section of the hospital campus: not much to see, mostly rooftops and air conditioning units. Erik turned and started back in the direction from which he came.

About halfway down the corridor, a patient he'd never seen before occupied a room on the right. A large device kept the blankets elevated from their lower extremities. The face. It was soft and feminine. Jet-black hair splayed out over her pillow, and he paused.

Something about this woman was familiar. He wracked his brain, attempting to work out where he knew her from, but nothing clicked. It wasn't until he was about to walk away; it came to him. It was the cop who found him in Blood Alley. The same one who did the first watch on his room in ICU after the death threat. The first real cop. Al didn't count — he was only a security guard.

Erik took a few tentative steps into her room. "Hi. Remember me?"

Sadness filled her ebony eyes. She turned her head away from him.

He pulled over the chair and sat. He could wait her out. She sure looked like she needed a friend. His patience was rewarded about fifteen minutes later when she turned back. Those beautiful eyes were red and filled with tears.

"You're still here?"

"Yeah." He was going to add 'nothing better to do' but thought better of it. Not the proper way to offer sympathy or commiserate. Talk like that would get a water jug or something chucked at him.

"Bug off."

He leaned forward in his seat. "You look like you could use a friend."

"What I need is my leg back," she snapped.

Her reaction shocked him. He should go and leave her to it, but something compelled him to stay. Finally, he stammered, "I'm sorry. I don't know what to say. How? When?" Now that he had found his voice, the questions spewed forth.

Erik stood and walked to the window. His problems were minor compared to Hilary's. Gunmetal grey clouds hung low, and raindrops spattered against the glass. Lightning slashed across the darkened sky, followed by an ear-piercing crack of thunder. Despite two insulated windows with six inches of airspace between them, the noise was loud. Startled, he flinched.

"So why did they stick you in this ward? I would have thought you'd be in ICU or on a surgical floor."

"No beds, I guess."

At least she spoke to him. That was a start. He returned to the chair. "You know, if you didn't find me when you did, we wouldn't be having this conversation. I'd be in the morgue."

"Luck, I guess," she mumbled.

Not much of a response, but she acknowledged his statement. "Did you hear, after they lifted the police guard on my room, someone laced my methadone with heroin."

Hilary propped herself up on her elbows and furrowed her brow. "I've been stuck in the hospital, missing a good piece of my leg, and you want to know if I heard about your treatment being tampered with? You're unbelievable." She flopped back on the bed and clenched the sheets in her hands.

"Sorry, okay? Thought talking about something else might ease your pain."

"I'm going to count to ten, and if you're not out of here by the time I reach it, you'll regret it."

"But …"

"One," a pause, "two," another pause.

"All right, I'm going," he retorted. Right away, he regretted the way he responded to her. He walked into the corridor and leaned against the wall next to her door. "Stupid, stupid, stupid," he muttered and bashed the back of his head against the heavily painted cement block wall in time with the words.

"Erik, are you still out there? I'm sorry. I shouldn't take my anger out on you. Come back in, please? I promise to behave and not chuck anything at you." She waited for his reply. Nothing. She called him again.

Five minutes elapsed before he appeared in the doorway. Some time since, Hilary did her last stint of guard duty, and now, he had shaved his head. It suited him. Put on a bit of weight, too. His hazel eyes sparkled with life, unlike when she first saw him after he regained consciousness. Then, they were dull and lifeless.

"Can I ask you how it happened without getting my head taken off?" He approached the chair he sat in earlier.

"You'll probably want to sit for this."

Erik adjusted its positioning and sat. "Tell me," he said.

"Well, we, my partner and I attended a domestic. Just our luck, we were first on-site. Like a dummy, I didn't wait for the SWAT team to secure the scene. Things got out of hand, as they quite often do. The woman held against her will screamed, and I positioned myself to shoot the perp. Well, he shot me instead."

"Wow."

She wanted to smack him for his response but didn't. "I collapsed immediately. Luke, you remember my partner, he dragged me behind a tree to protect me from getting hit again while down and unable to defend myself."

"And the rest, as they say, is history."

Hilary shifted. Between catheters, IV lines, and being short one leg, she couldn't get comfortable, despite the egg crate-like foam between the sheets and the mattress placed there to prevent bedsores. She'd be stuck in bed until a member of the medical staff helped her escape the confines of the single bed with its sides elevated.

She and Erik sat in silence. Having someone in her room made her feel less alone. Less helpless. But, he wouldn't be in hospital much longer. He would be released and go back to his drug habit and life on the streets.

Nine

Vancouver General Hospital, West 12th Avenue, Vancouver

"Hello, Dunbar," a tall, broad-shouldered man said as he entered the room. He smiled as he spoke, creating laugh lines around his mouth and crow's feet at the corners of his eyes.

The insignia on his uniform said he was the Chief Constable of the Vancouver Police Department. He called her by name. Until that moment, Hilary didn't think he knew she existed. "Hi," she said. "Didn't expect a visit from you."

He pulled the plastic chair to the bedside. "That was a good bit of police work on your part, identifying the tattoo on the perp's hand from the surveillance camera images."

"Th-thank you."

"Thought you would like to know the guy who shot you turned out to be none other than Carlos Navarra's right-hand-man, Frank Billings. The woman he held hostage was his girlfriend, Wendy Richmond. The whole thing was a setup. She was in on that and fed your OD vic the pure, uncut heroin instead of his methadone. They were willing to do anything to keep Carlos from going down by eliminating the person, or persons, who fingered him."

"Wow."

"You're a member of the family. Don't you forget it."

Was she still? Was he here to tell her her days on the force were over?

He rubbed his temples and said, "You suffered a grievous injury. I'm afraid I don't envision you going back to active duty."

"Why not? I'll be fitted for a prosthesis soon."

"Not just that. What about your mental health? Being shot in the line of duty, speaking of which, there will be a sizeable compensation package due to you."

Angry, Hilary pushed the covers aside. "Why, because of this?" She pointed to the bandages swaddling her left leg from about six inches above her knee to roughly the same distance below. Then nothing. Only space where the rest of her limb should be.

Her superior stood and turned his head away from the bed. "If you're determined to remain with the force, you'll be consigned to a desk job or public relations, going into the schools, talking to the students and such."

"Absolutely not. I go back in the car with Luke. I trust him with my life, and I know he won't let anything happen to me. I would have bled out and died if not for him."

He spun around to face her and said, "And it's situations like that, that won't allow me to send you back into the field. You broke protocol, Dunbar. Consider yourself lucky you're still employed." With each word uttered, his voice grew louder.

"Get out," she screamed.

"At least give the other options a think. I'll see you again soon."

"Don't bother," she snapped.

The Chief Constable exited the room in silence. Alone, Hilary flopped back on the bed. The man didn't come right out and say her police career was over — at least in those words, but he might as well have. Desk job or public relations. Bah!

Soon, the reality of what he said began to sink in. Hilary Dunbar an amputee. Her agility and speed compromised. No artificial leg would return her to her old self. Even the ones with blades that athletes wore wouldn't work. Scorching hot tears escaped her eyes and rolled towards her ears. She turned on her side with her back to the door. What was there to live for if she couldn't go back to her old position? She might as well crawl in a hole and die.

About an hour later, a familiar voice said, "Hiya."

Hilary remained still. If Erik thought she was sleeping, he'd go away and leave her alone. She willed herself not to move. That was her only hope of maintaining her solitude, but her body revolted and shuddered. Footsteps raced around the bed. A hand reached out and stroked her face. His compassion made things worse, and her tears flowed again.

Erik took her hand in both of his then sat beside her. The bed shifted when he sat on it. In minutes, he pulled Hilary into a sitting position with her head buried in his chest and put his arms around her. "Go ahead and cry," he soothed, rubbing her back.

Her emotions were in turmoil. Everything she worked so hard for was gone. Her parents were so proud when she graduated from police college. Her mother was against her being a member of the force. Still, on graduation day, she beamed with pride watching her daughter accept her diploma. Hilary followed in her father's, grandfather's and uncles' footsteps when she became a cop. Most were gone now. Her grandfather received a special commendation for his part in the arrest of a notorious gang leader.

What would she get from the force? Likely nothing. She already received her award. Leg lost below the knee, and with that, her job, not to mention, she'd be hauled in front of a panel to determine if she was negligent. Standard procedure they told her. She discharged her firearm — nothing to worry about.

Some days her missing leg itched like crazy. Other days a burning pain filled the space. Never anything excruciating but rather a gnawing pain like a toothache.

A young woman with long auburn hair entered Hilary's room and closed the door behind her. "I thought we could spend some time chatting."

"Who are you?" Hilary went back to staring at the ceiling. If she focussed long enough, the pattern in the ceiling tiles moved. Except for the lack of colour, it was like a kaleidoscope.

"Gillian Powell. I'm the psychiatrist on the ward," she said, extending her hand.

"What does that have to do with me and the price of tomatoes?"

"You've experienced severe trauma." The physician pulled the chair into a position along the bed near the foot. "You're no doubt, angry and confused. Maybe even in denial. You might put your emotions in perspective if you talked to someone."

"I don't want to, as you said it, put my emotions in perspective." Hilary pushed the button on the rail and raised the head of the bed. "What I want is my leg back. I want my career back, and since I can't have either, I might as well be dead. Nothing left to look forward to."

"What about family? Friends?"

"My mum is unable to travel. She's all I've got left." A tear rolled down her cheek, and she dashed it away.

"I'm sorry. Times like this, you need your mother. What about friends?"

"Just the members of the force. My partner, Luke. They're more family than anything."

"Have they come to see you?"

If only this nosey woman would leave. Hilary did not want to talk to her, but her soft voice and mannerisms made the answers spew out involuntarily. "Luke's been good about coming. The Chief Constable was in once, and that was one time too many. Told me I would never go back to active duty."

"Anyone else?"

Did she dare mention her visits with Erik? Probably not a smart idea. At least not by name. Change the subject? That would work. "I miss my dog."

"Oh?"

"She's a German Shepherd pup. A police dog school failure."

"Too bad. Where is the animal now?"

"Luke took her to his house the night I got shot. Xena has been staying with his family."

"That's nice. I could arrange for canine visits. Would you like that?"

"I'd love it. But how?"

"You leave it to me." With that, the psychiatrist stood, shook Hilary's hand and left.

Hilary didn't want to raise her hopes over the possibility of a visit from Xena. Just the time she did that, it wouldn't happen as the doctor said, and her dreams would be shattered. No, best to remain skeptical. If she did, she wouldn't be hurt when things didn't happen as promised.

Ten

Vancouver General Hospital, West 12th Avenue, Vancouver

"Erik, could you stay behind, please?"

He turned back towards his counsellor as the others left the huge room after group therapy.

"Your time here at Vancouver General is coming to an end. You've done extremely well," Paul said.

"Crap, I won't be safe on the outside. Navarra or his boys will be after me. They'll kill me when they find me. No. I have to stay." Erik's heart raced. No way he could be anywhere other than here. He was clean — on methadone, but no longer on heroin. If he were released, he would fall back into his old habits. All it would take would be to run into one of his druggie pals, and he knew he wouldn't be able to resist. He couldn't tell his counsellor that.

"Sorry, it's not up to me. The order came from above. We need the bed for others."

The following morning, Erik found himself in one of the

psychiatrist's offices. In addition to the young female mental health practitioner, Doctor Singh and another man were in attendance. Certificates lined the walls. The nameplate on her desk read Gillian Powell. Practically enough letters followed her surname to be its own alphabet. Yet, she looked young enough to be barely out of high school.

"Sit down," she said as she perched on the corner of her desk in front of him. Her auburn hair cascaded over her shoulder, and she swept it back in one fluid motion.

The men stood nearby.

Erik's eyes flicked back and forth between the two men. The doctor was familiar to him, but he had never laid eyes on the other guy at all. He was a bear of a man. Well over six feet tall and barrel-chested with thick, bushy eyebrows that almost met on the bridge of his nose. His otherwise black hair showed tinges of grey at the temples. The sleeves of his shirt stretched over the enormous muscles in his upper arms.

"We're pleased with your progress here, so much so that we're ready to release you into the community. You will continue your therapy at Vancouver Coastal Health's Onsite facility on East Hastings."

"But ..."

"Onsite is primarily for the folks who are using the supervised injection site on the ground floor. You'll have access to counsellors, mental health practitioners, as well as doctors and nurses — twelve private rooms. Once you're stable, you'll move to the third floor. You'll continue your recovery there. Consider it a re-entry house. You'll be supported in getting in touch with your family, if you want, and in your job search. What could be better?"

Erik squirmed in his chair. "What about my methadone treatment?"

"The city has numerous facilities where you can go for your treatment. You'll need an initial prescription, which I'll provide," said the psychiatrist, "and it will be up to you where you have it filled."

"There are two clinics within a five-minute walk of our shelter," the big man said.

Until then, he remained silent. The man did have a voice. Not at all what Erik expected. He assumed with the guy's stature; the voice would be deep and booming, but no. It was higher-pitched and almost feminine. He wasn't, was he?

"Forgive me. I never introduced you. Erik, this is Des Norton, the supervisor of Onsite.

The man nodded.

Erik rubbed his hand on his recently shaved head. "East Hastings. The name sounds familiar."

"In Gastown. Stone's throw from the Police Museum and Archives."

The blood rushed from Erik's face. Not all that far from Blood Alley either. "I can't go back — too many dealers and users in that area. I should know. I was one. User, that is." He felt the need to clarify the fact he was one of the latter as opposed to one of the former. "Put me in that place, and I'll be back on the smack in no time. You got to place me somewhere else."

"I'm sorry, Erik. The decision has been made. You'll be admitted to Onsite. It will be good for you to face your demons and rise above them."

Hilary turned at the sound of police boots on the tile floor. "How did you get in here with Xena?"

"Not hard. Walked in, and here we are."

"No hassles?"

"Nope. At least not yet. Hospitals are getting more lenient when it comes to patients and their pets." Luke lifted the German Shepherd and placed her on the bed. Despite Xena's usual rambunctious and overly friendly behaviour, which led to her failure of police dog training, she settled in beside Hilary and rested her head on her thigh.

"Isn't that only for palliative patients?"

"Dunno. Besides, what difference does it make? Bringing Xena to see you put a smile on your face. That's what counts."

She stroked the animal's soft coat. It hadn't been all that long since she was admitted to hospital, but now, it seemed a lifetime ago since she cuddled with her dog like this.

Erik left the psychiatrist's office disheartened. This ward had become home to him: the patients, his friends. Family even. Soon he would be leaving them. Hilary had to find out. It was up to him to inform her. She couldn't find out from someone on the floor. Her state of mind since losing her leg was tenuous, at best. Would another upset push her past the brink?

He walked into her hospital room, contemplating how to bring the subject up. A uniformed cop sat in the chair he usually occupied, and a long-haired puppy showered Hilary with slobbery kisses.

At Erik's entrance, the policeman stood and lifted the dog off the bed. Hilary's smile lit up the room. This was the happiest she'd been since he first stumbled across her.

"You remember my partner, Luke," she said, "and this fifty-odd pound fur ball is my police dog failure, Xena. She's been staying with Luke and his family since my incident."

He nodded in acknowledgement.

"This is Erik. You probably don't remember him. He's changed a lot since I discovered him in Blood Alley."

Luke glared. His unspoken words spoke volumes. The man clipped the leash to the dog's collar, never once taking his eyes off Erik.

The scrutiny made him uncomfortable. His palms became clammy, and beads of sweat formed on his forehead. He was no longer the same person he was back then. He had changed. Nearly dying from tainted heroin did that to a person. He walked around the bed and stared out the window.

Pressure on his thigh made him seek out the cause. Xena stood on her back legs, her front ones on his. Erik reached down and scratched the top of her head between her ears. His actions made the dog jump and twist and beg for more.

He slid down the wall until he was on the floor. No sooner did he settle than the German Shepherd clambered on his lap and showered him with kisses.

"She doesn't normally take to strangers. There must be something special about you," said Hilary.

Luke's stony expression didn't change.

"You're going to have to come up with alternate arrangements for Xena," said Luke. "Kim wants her gone. She can't cope with her."

"She can't go back to my place. There's no one to look after her." Hilary shifted her position on the bed.

"What about the kennels?"

"Never," she spat.

"Why don't I take her?" Erik said. "She seems to like me. Never had a pet growing up. I need her as much as she needs someone."

"But you're still a patient. The hospital won't let her stay on the ward."

"Not straight away. After I'm released, I mean. This girl would give me a reason to stay focussed on my recovery."

"Living rough in the streets? Absolutely not."

"Not the streets. Arrangements already made to admit me to Onsite. Once I'm settled there."

Hilary hesitated. "Maybe."

Luke scowled. She was thinking of letting this drug addict look after her dog. The hound of the Baskervilles as his wife referred to the mutt. Was this guy someone from Hilary's past? She told him about her desire to become a cop not long after they partnered with each other. Said it ran in her family, grandfather, father and uncles were cops, but never said anything else about who she was or what made her what she was and is today. That chapter of her life, other than law enforcement, remained closed to him.

Onsite. That place was over the Supervised Injection facility on East Hastings. Of all areas to house Erik. Would he keep his word and remain focussed on getting and staying straight? The neighbourhood was sketchy at the best of times.

She and Luke patrolled it regularly. Homeless people and drug addicts loitered in front of buildings. Numerous shouts to reports of robbery, soliciting and drug deals.

Still, the facility had an excellent reputation for helping people with their recovery and getting them back on their feet. If only it were in a better part of town. Someplace less seedy. And this place had to come up some to even rank that high.

Eleven

Vancouver General Hospital, West 12th Avenue, Vancouver

"You let me know when and where, and I'll bring the dog around there right away." The opportunity to get Xena out of his house filled Luke with joy. Strange as the exchange between Hilary and Erik was, from his perspective, she liked the guy. Even more curious, she seemed to trust him. With the dog gone, he might be able to talk Kim out of moving forward with divorce proceedings. A lot happened on the day of the shooting. Was his wife's worry the catalyst that brought everything to a head?

"I'm not sure about this," said Hilary. Her eyes darted back and forth between the men.

"I am," said Luke. "Kim wants the dog out of the house. You don't want to put her in a kennel. Can we say serendipity?"

"I don't know. I'll have to think about it."

"What's to think about?" said Erik. "I love dogs. She seems to have taken a shine to me."

Hilary slumped back in her bed. Was letting Erik take over Xena's care the right thing to do? From all accounts, her dog liked the man. Likewise, he took a liking to her. It was apparent Luke never wanted the role of dog sitting, albeit most of it fell to his wife because she was home more than he was.

Luke practically walked on air when he and Xena left Hilary's room. Let the devil dog be someone else's worry. She chewed through one of Kim's shoes, and a rubber boot belonging to Emma and who knew what else during her short stay in his home.

A more apt name for the beast was Beelzebub, Lucifer, Mephistopheles, Satan or anything else related to hell. Naming the creature after a fictional warrior princess who fought against evil, to him, was an oxymoron.

After he pulled in the drive, he opened the gate, unclipped the leash, and put the dog in the back yard. The latch snapped into position, ensuring the captivity of said animal.

"Excellent news hon," Luke yelled as he walked in the front door. His jovial mood came to an abrupt end when he spotted his wife sitting on the end of the sofa, twisting a tissue in her hands. It was wet. She had been crying and by all accounts still was. He rushed to her side.

"Hey babe, what's wrong?" He took her hands in his.

"I don't want a divorce. It's just all that happened that day, and now Hilary is crippled.

"Don't let her hear you say that. She'll have your guts for garters for that kind of talk."

Kim turned to him. Her eyes were red and tear-filled. She still fiddled with the tissue in her hands despite his holding them. "You said you had great news when you came in the door. What is it?"

"Devil dog will be leaving soon." He couldn't put an exact date on the fiend's departure. It was dependent on Erik's release from the hospital.

"The giant hairball isn't that bad. I'm just not used to having a dog around and having to puppy-proof the house."

"Speaking of Xena, it's too quiet outside. I best check on her. I put her in the back yard when I got back from seeing Hilary in the hospital."

Luke went to the back door and into the closed-in porch. Xena stood in the centre of one of Kim's flower beds surrounded by flattened plants. He dashed out the door. A cursory inspection revealed nothing was broken off, so given time should recover. He herded the canine into the house.

Kim met him in the kitchen. "How badly are they damaged?" she asked.

"I think they'll come back. Looks like I won't be leaving Xena unattended out there anymore," he said, raking his fingers through his hair. Luke pointed to the doorway, and the dog slunk through to the small room off the living room where her bed was set up.

His hand behind his wife's back, he escorted her to the sofa.

"Do you think Hilary would like it if I went to see her?" she asked. "I remember meeting her at one of the Policeman's Balls. I liked her. When you first told me your partner was a woman, I was jealous, but I realize I have nothing to worry about on that front. She's professional. You're professional, and I trust you."

"She would love visitors. I don't think any of the guys have been in for a visit. Her injuries have put them off. They don't know what to say to her. Afraid of putting their size 10s where they shouldn't."

"I'm not sure I won't say anything wrong." She grabbed a tissue from the box on the end table and blew her nose.

"I'm glad you're feeling better. Don't be afraid to talk to me about my job. There might be some things I can't tell you, or go into detail about, but I'll be as forthcoming as possible. Will that help put your fears to rest?"

She nodded.

Luke wrapped his arm around her shoulders and pulled her

to him.

Kim pulled back. "Should I take her something?"

"Sure, why not?"

"There's a Shoppers Drug Mart near the hospital. I'll stop in and pick up some toiletries for her before I visit."

The next morning, Kim took advantage of her husband being off duty for a few days and took the bus to the hospital to visit Hilary. Unsure what to do or say, the prospect made her nervous. She had only met the woman a few times at social functions or charity events the force sponsored. The last thing she wanted was to put her foot in it and say something to upset her.

Her first stop was at the Shoppers Drug Mart. She wandered through the aisles, debating what she might buy. In the end, Kim decided on personal care items — a new hairbrush, toothbrush, body wash, a pouf, and cosmetics.

Once she found out where Hilary's room was, she negotiated her way through the warren of corridors to the elevators. Beads of nervous sweat formed at her hairline and trickled down the back of her neck. Same with her armpits. Maybe this wasn't such a good idea. Even her palms were sweaty.

Outside the room, she paused, wiped her hands against her thighs, and hemmed. "H-hi," she said when she crept into the room. "You probably don't remember me."

Hilary frowned as she studied her. "Kim? Kim Stephanopoulos? Luke's wife, right?"

"Y-yes." No matter how hard she tried, she couldn't stop staring at the space where Hilary's lower left leg should be. "I thought you might like some company. Lukas is off today and looking after the girls, so I took advantage of the break," she finally said, bringing an end to the awkward silence. She leaned against the footboard of the bed to support herself.

"How are Luke and the girls? Leah and Emma isn't it?"

Kim nodded, terrified if she spoke out loud, she would say the wrong thing.

"Don't be nervous," Hilary said. "Do you think I could get my shoes at half price? As it is, I only need one from every pair." A smile tugged at the corners of her mouth.

The attempt at humour put Kim at ease. She pulled over the other chair and sat before wiping her palms on her thighs. This visit was far more complicated than she imagined.

"Brought you some things. The hospital provides some for you, but having your own is always nice. I hope I chose well." She passed the bag to Hilary.

"We first met at a Policeman's ball then you and Luke brought the girls to last year's kids' Christmas party. The one I got conned into being one of Santa's elves at," she said as she inspected the bag's contents.

"That was you? Wow." She stopped before saying something that might offend the woman in front of her. The costume, while not indecent, showed a substantial amount of leg. A shapely one at that. No more now. At least not in that kind of outfit. No way she could dress like that anymore. Not with only one leg. Even with an artificial limb, she doubted Hilary would do it. Her life going forward would be reduced to loose-fitting trousers to hide the fact she was an amputee.

"Thanks. How did you know this was the brand I used?" She extracted a tube of mascara from the bag.

"Just a guess. Excellent one at that." Kim wiped her sweaty palms on her thighs again. "I always think if you don't look like a bag of dirt, you won't feel like one." Wonderful. Really put her foot in it with that comment. She sighed with relief when Hilary chuckled.

"I'll let you know how it works for me." She dug through the bag again and came up with a package of hair elastics and a brush. With an elastic hairband around her hand, Hilary brushed her hair and pulled it up into a ponytail with a pair of muscular arms. Not a single sign of fat on the girl. She was fit.

Kim was far from fat, but seeing Hilary's leanness made her lament her less than perfect curves. "You must go to the gym a lot?" What a dumb question. The woman must think she was pathetic.

"Used to go every day. Sometimes twice a day. Won't be

doing that again anytime soon."

"Why not? I'll bet even though you're stuck in here for a while; you're still more fit than most of the ones there."

"For a start, you can't do squats and lunges with only one leg. Maybe the squats, but nothing else that requires two."

"Don't be a defeatist. You've not tried it. You'll be fitted for another leg soon if you haven't already been."

Hilary scowled at her.

Kim took it as her queue to leave. "Hope you get lots of use out of those things," she said as she walked towards the door.

Hilary's weak attempt at humour during Kim's visit didn't help her emotional state once she was on her own again. She straightened her left leg, what remained of it, and punched her thigh. Worst of all, her situation was self-inflicted. Had she waited for the SWAT team to arrive and secure the premises, she wouldn't have been shot and end up having her leg amputated. Her impetuous move would live with her for the rest of her life. If it continued like this, she might as well kill herself and get it over.

Alone now, Hilary wheeled herself closer to the overbed table. She spun it around, so it was in front of the chair, pulled open the vanity tray and erected the mirror. Still too high for her to see, she lowered the unit until she could.

A tear ran down her cheek, and she dashed it away. Hilary didn't want to see herself cry. Bag upended, she dumped the contents into the tray, slammed it shut, and pushed the wheeled piece of furniture away. It bounced off the metal bedside table with a clatter. Why would she need cosmetics? She did not need them. No one would want to date a cop, let alone a one-legged ex-cop.

Erik enjoyed his visits with Hilary. Befriending her was the best thing that had happened to him in a long time. He couldn't believe his luck when she agreed to let him look after

Xena once the hospital released him to the Onsite rehabilitation centre.

The methadone kept his heroin withdrawal symptoms at bay. Since he started the treatment, his desire to inject himself full of illegal street drugs and spend his life stoned disappeared. Funny how his outlook changed, now he was straight. He wanted it to stay that way.

When he first started treatments, no one said how long he would continue on them. Leaflets he'd picked up in the hospital spoke of varying lengths of time. Some stated as little as ninety days, while others a year of methadone maintenance was more successful, and depending on the addict; the treatment could go on for many years.

Guilt over the torment he put his family through periodically overwhelmed him. He was never the perfect child. That title belonged to his sister, Serenity. She worked hard at school — he ditched classes as often as possible. With their father being an alcoholic and their mother unable to manage with two kids and a drunk, Erik turned to drugs as a coping mechanism. His sibling never touched a drop of the drink or took drugs — not so much as an aspirin. She was strong. Much stronger than he.

His parents always reminded him of that. 'Why can't you be more like your sister? You could do so much better if you applied yourself.' Rich, coming from a work-shy alcoholic. Vague memories from his early childhood were of his father working regularly. Although they weren't wealthy, they were far better off. Then everything fell apart. The man lost his job and turned to the booze.

As a small child, Erik never understood the reason. When he got older and overheard snippets of conversations about the good old days, he was able to put the pieces together. His father worked at Goodyear Tire and Rubber until the factory closed in 1987.

What became of his family? Were his parents still alive? They didn't have a phone before he ran off and doubted they did now. His father was verbally abusive when he had a snootful but never raised a hand to them. If anyone deserved a thrashing, it was Erik. His mother kept to herself and stayed in the bedroom often and for long periods — no doubt avoiding her drunken lout of a husband.

Erik lied and stole from the family every chance he got. At first, he started out using marijuana and gradually worked his way into heroin. To this day, how he got from the Toronto neighbourhood where he grew up to the streets of Vancouver baffled him. The destruction of his sister, Serenity's prized possession — a stuffed panda bear their father dragged home after setting up the midway of the Canadian National Exhibition was down to him. One of the few jobs the man managed not to lose.

Serenity, she would go places. Smart and determined, she would succeed. But at what? If only he could contact her. Would she want to have anything to do with him after the things he did when they were children? Not likely.

Twelve

Vancouver General Hospital, West 12th Avenue, Vancouver

"Gather up your things, hon," a plump, middle-aged nurse said when she entered Hilary's room. "It's moving day."

"Moving? Where to?"

"Found you a bed on a regular floor. You don't need to be in here."

"But …"

"No buts." The woman shifted, and her photo ID turned enough Hilary could read the lettering. Her name was Pat.

"I have friends in this ward. How will they be able to visit me if I'm not here?"

"They won't. Sorry, hon. A secure unit is this. You won't be able to see anyone from here until they're released."

The nurse bustled around the room opening and closing doors and drawers gathering Hilary's things and putting them in a green garbage bag she pulled out of her tunic pocket.

Things had gone from bad to the absolute worst. When she told the nurse she had friends, Erik was the only one. She had to notify him before it was too late.

"What's going on here?"

Did the guy have ESP or something? The thought of making him aware of her change in rooms had popped into her head only seconds before. "They're moving me out of here to a different floor."

"I'll still come and see you."

"You can't. With this being a secure unit, you won't be able to." A tear ran down her cheek, and she dashed it away before Erik saw her crying.

"You should have a phone in your room, so we'll at least be able to talk on the phone." He reached over and took her hand in both of his.

Hilary nodded.

Pat plopped the bag containing Hilary's things in her lap and grabbed the wheelchair's handles. "Let's get moving. Haven't got all day."

Erik held her hand the entire way to the security doors. "at least let me know your room number. I'll be out of here soon, so will stop and visit you before I leave."

"Okay," said Hilary, her voice filled with emotion.

"I'll visit you every day, promise."

"Don't make promises you can't keep."

The nurse swiped her card, and the doors to the unit opened. She pushed Hilary through.

Erik raked his fingers across his head. He could step through those doors and follow them, but his luck the alarms would go off. As the doors closed, he glimpsed them rounding a corner farther down the corridor. Hilary sat slumped in the chair. His heart broke, seeing her in this state. He understood the reason behind moving her but didn't like it. She was as good for him as he was for her. They were each other's rocks.

After the locks latched, Erik remained in the hall staring at the solid grey barrier. Eventually, he turned and schlepped back to his room. Despite patients occupying almost every room, the unit was empty without Hilary. He never took the time to know anyone else, not that he had any desire. Most were worse off than he was and kept to themselves.

He flopped on his bed, folded his arms behind his head and stared at the ceiling.

Canary yellow walls greeted Hilary when Pat wheeled her into her new room. Of all the colours, this was the one she liked the least. At least being private, she didn't have to share with anyone.

The nurse placed the bag on the bed. "I'll leave you to get settled. If you need anything, holler."

"Can you tell my friend my room number?"

"Do it yourself," she said, pointing to a spot in the corner. "There's a phone on your bedside table."

Rude response to her request. "Is there a directory with the numbers for the different wards?"

"Dial through to switchboard, and they'll transfer you."

Hilary was about to say something else, but except for her, the room was empty. She wheeled herself to the window and set the brakes on her chair. Using the arms, she raised herself to a standing position and leaned her elbows on the sill.

The grey skies matched her mood. Her life took a nosedive the day of the shooting. If not for Erik's visits and her beloved dog, she would have given up all hope. It was strange to think a drug addict and a cop could be friends, but in her case, their friendship worked. Erik kept her going. There might have been some ulterior motive on his part. Maybe helping her helped him. She didn't care. His visits, sometimes not wanted, were what she needed.

She was in shape before the incident. Some of her upper body strength from working out remained. Otherwise, she wouldn't have been able to push herself into a standing position. Now, she felt like an ungainly flamingo standing on one leg. The only difference, the big pink bird, had the option of putting its other foot on the ground.

Still peeved at the nurse's attitude when she asked the woman to update Erik, Hilary sighed. She dropped into the chair, released the brakes and wheeled to the phone. Five minutes later, the staff in the Mental Health and Substance Use unit had her information. She hoped someone would relay the details to Erik.

Next, she had to let Luke know she was in a different room. She called the police department, and her call was transferred throughout the building to colleagues and superiors, all asking the same questions. 'How are you? When are you coming back?' Her pat answer to both was 'fine and as soon as you will have me.' After the number of times she repeated the phrase, it became old.

In the back of her mind, she knew she would never return to active duty, which was what she wanted more than anything. She left her new contact information with the duty sergeant and hung up the phone, hoping he would pass the details on. Maybe even some of her fellow officers would visit her.

Des arrived at the hospital to take Erik to his new accommodations. Once his meagre belongings were gathered up, the Onsite supervisor signed the release documents, and they exited the secure unit.

Whether the man granted his request remained to be seen, but he posed the question anyway. "Can we make a stop first? I want to say goodbye to someone before we leave."

The man wrinkled his nose. "Long as you're quick."

They stepped into the elevator in silence.

The expanse and layout of Vancouver General created a challenge to navigate from one ward to another if you were unsure of where you had to go. Some time, and a lot of questions later, they finally found Hilary's new room.

"I couldn't go without seeing you first," said Erik as he stepped through the door.

Her ebony eyes were glassy with tears. "I'm glad you did."

He walked to the bed and took her hand in his. "I'll be back first chance."

"Did you mean what you said about looking after Xena? Will they let you keep her there?"

Erik leaned down closer to her. "Don't care what they say.

I'll look after her. She's my service dog. She's what's going to keep me clean."

A smile tugged at the edges of Hilary's mouth. "I'll let Luke know," she whispered.

"Come on. We've got to go," said Des.

"Okay. Keep your hair on." Erik turned back to Hilary. "Bye. See you soon."

Des opened the trunk of his dark green Toyota Corolla, and Erik tossed in his backpack then climbed into the passenger seat. Once he stowed the gear, the Onsite supervisor squeezed in behind the wheel. For such a big man, the car was small.

"I'll drive you by both clinics, and you can decide which one you prefer to use for your methadone prescription." He pulled the car out of the parking lot and worked his way to Cambie Street.

"Sure." Erik stared out the window. Sailboats bobbed on their moorings in the water below the bridge over False Creek. This was the first time he passed through this part of the city. In his previous life, he languished in his drug-induced state in the area surrounding Blood Alley in Gastown. Straight ahead, a wall of high-rises rose from the ground. So far, the most picturesque vista was the bay with all the boats and ferries.

He told Hilary before leaving the hospital, Xena would be well looked after. He couldn't; no wouldn't let her down.

"That chick, she's, she's the cop that was shot?"

"Yeah," said Erik, his eyes focussed on his surroundings.

"How did you meet up with her? You were in a secure unit."

"So was she, for a while. Shortage of beds, I guess."

Des nodded. "You looked closer than two people who just met."

"If you must know, she saved my life. If not for her finding me in Blood Alley when she did, I would be dead."

"Yup, that you would."

Des slowed the car and pulled to the curb. "Here's Pender Community."

The two-storey building stood sandwiched between two taller ones. The neighbourhood seemed harmless, unlike some of the others where Erik had spent time.

"Seen enough?"

"For now."

Once they were moving again, Des said, "I'll take you by Onsite and then down to Doc-Side."

Ahead, a humongous Chinese-style archway rose above the street; its outermost bases on each sidewalk flanked by an Oriental lion.

Soon after Des made the right turn on to East Hastings, he brought the car to a stop across the street from a dark green, drab storefront. The upper two floors of the building wore a coat of brown, most of which had peeled away. The same shade of green covered the window trim and cornice of the structure.

"Supervised injection site downstairs. Accommodations upstairs. Third floor is the transitional unit."

Homeless people with their paltry belongings slept rough on the sidewalks. Two people stoned out of their minds on something leaned against the building. An oversize black sign with white lettering painted on a grey wall read the Balmoral Hotel. Fancier signage adorned the front façade of the structure. Graffiti tags covered the fronts of many of the buildings. Another hotel, The Regent, was almost straight across the road. Erik decided he would avoid both.

There was so much to take in on this block. People loitered in front of the Four Directions Community Economic & Employment Development Centre. Farther along, yet another hotel. This time, The Empress and it looked as bad as the previous two. Construction sites among the older buildings gave hope that the area was emerging from decline. A faded Robin Hood Flour sign painted on a brick wall showed its age over which was the name of the hotel, although that signage was harder to read.

Farther down the street, Des squeezed the car into a bay. "Here we are. Doc-Side is in here."

Erik scrutinized the building. The last block to block and a half was an improvement over the previous ones. Still, many places on the other side of the street fared badly over the years. Boarded-up storefronts and others with their pull-down security doors in the locked position spoke volumes.

"Well? Pender Community or here?"

It was a no-brainer. Erik's mind was long-since made up. "Not here."

"I was hoping you'd say that." Des paused. "That's not going to work." He bashed the steering wheel with the palm of his hand. "Neither one of these places is open on weekends. Hang on a minute." He pried his cellphone from his pocket, punched in some numbers and waited. "Got Erik Layne with me. We're parked out front of Doc-Side, and I just remembered this place and Pender aren't open on weekends. What's the closest location to Onsite where he'll be living."

Silence.

Des rooted for a pen and paper. "Downtown Community Health Clinic on Powell. I know where that is. Thanks." He turned to Erik. "Change of plans. Still a short hop away from where you'll be staying, and they're available on weekends and stat holidays."

They were moving again. Once back in traffic, Des turned left at the next intersection. This street appeared to be residential on one side and industrial on the other. Just before the restricted access to the freight yards, he turned left again. Once they passed through the traffic lights at the next block, he pulled over to the left of the one way street. "Right in there. We'll continue up this way so you can figure out how you want to go back and forth. Seven days a week."

"Looks all right."

"You can cut through Oppenheimer Park. It only goes one block west and south to East Cordova, so you still have another block to go to get back. I recommend you stay on Powell here, or if you do cut through the park, carry on to Main Street. Then only half a block on East Hastings to return to home sweet home." He chuckled and pointed as he drove, indicating the streets.

When they reached the street mentioned, Des turned left, and they continued to Onsite. After rounding the last corner, he said, "And whatever you do, stay out of that alley."

Within the confines of the narrow passage, garbage littered the street. Dumpsters lined one side, and homeless people had set up beside and in between them. Not a place Erik planned to visit anytime soon — if ever. "No problem with that. I wouldn't be caught dead in that place."

Des's mouth curled into a smile. "Glad to hear. We'll settle you in your room; then, I'll set up your prescription with the clinic. It'll be ready for you today."

"Good." How to bring up the fact he promised to keep Xena until Hilary's release from the hospital. Fudge things and say she's his service dog? Fess up and say he promised to look after her dog until she's out of the hospital? Either way, he would have the German Shepherd with him.

Erik entered his small but clean room. A single bed lined the wall below the window. A clean towel, housecoat and slippers had been laid out on top of the blankets. A table lamp sat atop a nightstand that had a small drawer at the top and a larger compartment below. Farther along that wall stood a five-drawer dresser. It would be ample room for him and Xena. He couldn't wait for someone to bring her to him.

Practicalities needed to be worked out if he was going to use public transit to travel to the hospital from here. Not having a watch, he had to depend on the accuracy of the clock in Des's car.

They had checked out the other methadone clinics on their way here. Between that, construction and traffic, he figured they drove around for about twenty minutes. How long would it take him to walk the distance? How much would the bus fare cost? He had no money and no means of making any. Muddle through today and see what the next one brought. Could Erik even find his way back to Vancouver General?

Onsite allowed him a certain extent of freedom. He opened the drawer in the nightstand. Leaflets on services provided by the facility and a well-thumbed Bible occupied the space. He wouldn't need those.

The opportunity to tell the staff at Onsite about Xena before her arrival never arose.

Des pointed at the dog. "What is *that* doing in here?"

The tone of the man's voice and the emphasis he put on the one word said he was not the least bit pleased.

"She's his service dog," said Luke.

The supervisor looked at one man then the other.

"I've only got a few minutes. I'll grab the rest of Xena's stuff out of the van and be right back." Luke retreated out the door.

With the area surrounding Onsite, logic dictated he wouldn't want to leave his vehicle unattended for too long. Anything could happen.

Minutes later, he returned with the dog's toys, bed and bag of food. "Here you go. Don't have her vest with me. One of the girls must have taken it to her room," he said and winked.

During his stay in the Mental Health and Substance Use ward, Erik spent much of his time reading. In one of the magazines there, he read an article about the use of service dogs for recovering drug addicts. Xena took a liking to him, so taking care of her was the perfect solution to everyone's problem. Hilary didn't have to worry about her dog. Luke got his house back to normal.

The supervisor left, shaking his head.

"Thanks for that," said Erik.

"Don't mention it."

"In time, she'll need something to prove she's a service dog."

"Leave it with me. I'll come up with something. Get Kim on it. She's pretty handy with a sewing machine. And with the devil dog being out of the house, she'll whip up something in a heartbeat." Luke grinned. "Okay, gotta go. Say hi to Hilary for me the next time you visit her."

Xena walked to her bed, circled in one direction, then the other, and dropped with a thud. Almost instantly, she was sound asleep. Erik needed to find a place to store her food, where the animal couldn't get into the bag. She was still small enough; even if she stood on her back legs, she couldn't reach the top of the dresser, so that's where he put it. While the dog snored, he left his room and found a bathroom where he filled her dish with cold water.

When the time came to go for his methadone treatment, he would take Xena with him. Find out how she walked on the leash. That would be something else she would need — a proper harness. Hopefully, Luke's wife would incorporate that into the garment. That is if Luke convinced her to create one.

Des poked his head around the door. "Your 'scrip is at the clinic. Will be ready for you when you arrive." He handed a sheet of paper to Erik. "Show this at reception, and they'll look after you."

Erik took the proffered document and shoved it into his back jeans pocket.

A loud sigh came from the dog's bed.

"She won't be any trouble. Give you my word."

"Better not be."

The clinic on Powell Street closed at five o'clock during the week. The glowing red numerals on the digital clock in his room read four-fifteen. With the length of the drive from the health centre back to Onsite, Erik estimated it would take him about twenty minutes to walk the distance. Probably longer with the dog.

With the collar and leash on Xena, the two left his room. Erik moved closer to the street at the foot of the alley Des told him to avoid. He empathized with the homeless, having been in the same situation himself. Now that he had a second chance, he didn't want to destroy it and end up back on the streets.

Nervous perspiration dampened his armpits and the back of his neck. His eyes darted back and forth, searching for anyone who had anything to do with Navarra. If he encountered one or more, he had to be ready to run. Would Hilary's dog protect him?

Xena walked well on the leash — stayed to heel and never tugged. Well, that was until they turned the corner, and she sniffed the blanket of someone sleeping rough by the curb. A gentle tug and she rejoined him.

He contemplated the route Des told him about using Oppenheimer Park but carried on directly to Powell Street determining the most direct way would be prudent. On the way home after his treatment, and time wasn't crucial, the two would go through the park. Xena might like to have a wander in the grass.

On the baseball diamond in one corner of the green space, stood a village of dome tents. A cluster within the perimeter of the backstop and others further away. A motorhome and camper parked on the adjacent side street. Homeless? Sit-in? Rather than waste valuable time here, he continued to the clinic where he would receive his dose of methadone.

Only one more block to go. This was a rather pleasant walk. Two times a day back and forth, he would be in shape in no time. His four-legged companion seemed to enjoy the outing, and Hilary wouldn't be in condition to take her out for quite some time.

A sour-faced receptionist greeted Erik when he entered the Community Health Clinic. She scowled at him, then the dog. Paperwork extracted from his jeans pocket, he passed it over to her. The woman's expression never changed. She made a quick phone call, handed his prescription back to him and pointed through a set of double doors.

Once past the gauntlet, he found the location where he would receive his treatment. This time the healthcare worker was a guy.

In her eyes, Hilary failed as a cop. Acted recklessly and

could have easily had her partner, the father of two little girls, shot as well. If she were home, she would be alone, and no one checking in on her. She could kill herself, and no one would know.

Her depression scared her. Was she so desperate she contemplated taking her life? She flopped back in her bed and stared at the ceiling. If she were to make such a drastic move, what method would she use? Pills? Gun? Knife? The first option would be pain-free. Shooting, slashing or stabbing herself would cause a great deal of pain. And, if she failed, then she would be relegated to a life of further isolation.

How many days had it been since Erik left the hospital? One? Two? More? Each day followed the same routine, so they blended into one. He promised to look after Xena. Would he? Or would he sell her for drug money?

"Get dressed. We're going out. Cleared it at the desk."

Erik and her German Shepherd pup stood in the doorway.

"I don't have any clothes other than these hospital issue gems."

"Never thought of that. Can I pick up some things for you from your house?"

"I'd love it, but Luke still has my keys ... I think." Did she want Erik in her house going through her things? Could he be trusted? Xena didn't seem any worse for wear, but things could change.

She opened the vanity drawer in the overbed table. No house keys. Next, she opened the drawer in the bedside table. A pink lanyard lay in a pile with keys, and a purple plastic hippo attached. Hilary plucked them out and handed them over. "Something practical and my pair of Nike trainers."

A silence fell between them. She only needed one shoe. Why did she refer to them as a pair? Habit presumably.

"What's your address? I'll go collect some things for you and be back in a flash."

"499 East 7th Avenue. You know where that is?"

"Rough idea."

Hilary scribbled down the most direct route from the hospital to her home. "Here. It's still about half an hour each way on foot."

"You're all right."

The desire to escape the confines of the hospital overwhelmed Hilary periodically, and this was one of those occasions.

Erik consulted the directions and headed off. Xena trotted beside him. It was like she knew she was going home. The instructions were easy to follow. After an enjoyable stroll, with only one poop and scoop stop, he found himself in front of Hilary's house.

Stairs. Seven from street level to the front door, then a full flight to reach the top floor of her house. In her current state, she could never come home. There wasn't enough room to build a wheelchair ramp, not that she would thank him for it. Crutches? She might be able to navigate going up with them, but coming back down could be disastrous. Sadness washed over him.

The dog gave a tug, and the two ascended the front steps. Erik unlocked the deadbolt. To open the door, he had to put his shoulder against it and shove hard. A humongous stack of mail on the floor caused the issue. Before going any further, he unclipped the leash from Xena's collar, and she bounded off.

While the dog explored her home turf, he separated the mail into three piles — proper mail that required attention, store flyers, and personalized junk. Even with this initial sort, some of what he deemed relevant might turn out to be nothing of consequence. That stack would go to the hospital and Hilary could sort through it.

Straight ahead stood the staircase to the upper floor. Beyond it, the open door revealing the kitchen. Erik went there first and found a plastic bag for the mail. The ivory painted walls in the hall, living room and dining area contrasted with the dark stained trim, newel post and stair treads. The risers and spindles were the same colour as the walls.

An overstuffed sofa lined the wall under the front window. Along the far wall stood a closed roll-top desk with a stool under the edge of it.

This house was neat and tidy, aside from a layer of dust because no one was home to clean. Such a contrast from his home growing up. Most of the housework had been done by his older sister, especially after their father lost his job.

No time to dwell on the past. Erik came to get Hilary some clothes so he could take her out for walks. Xena charged down the stairs and skidded to a stop near his feet. She cocked her head and looked at a spot near the steps, then back at him with a confused expression. Was that the area her bed occupied?

On the second level, he went into a bedroom filled with white princess-like furniture. Standing in front of the dresser, he pulled open the uppermost drawer. A wave of relief washed over him when it was empty. Inside the closet, he found a medium-sized hardshell suitcase with wheels. He pulled it out and placed it on the bed. Hilary's clothing would go in it.

The bedroom overlooking the street in front of the house held a Queen-size bed with antique metal head and footboards. A four-drawer mirrored dresser stood along the wall to the left — a tall six-drawer one across from it, next to a set of closet doors.

T-shirts, sweatshirts and pants all neatly folded were extracted from the furniture and taken into the other room. Now it was time for the part he dreaded. When he first mentioned collecting some clothes for her, underwear was the furthest thing from his mind. He pulled open a drawer and reached into the mirrored dresser. Socks. Erik exhaled, not realizing he'd been holding his breath all along. Mated sports socks in assorted colours lay within the wooden confines. Not bothering to count out individual pairs, he grabbed a handful and put them with the other clothing he already collected.

Had Hilary forgotten about panties? Him having to go through her undies to bring some to her? Embarrassed, he cringed and turned away as he reached into the other small drawer next to the one where he found her socks and pulled out underpants. They weren't lacy, frilly, or girlie. Was that what he'd expected?

Heat rose to Hilary's cheeks. She touched one with the back of her hand. If it was as red as it was hot, she was redder than a beet. Why didn't she call Kim and ask her? Luke's wife would have done it. While it was sweet that Erik volunteered to bring her some clothing, it was embarrassing for them both. She picked up a magazine and fanned her face hoping to quash the blush but was unsuccessful.

He never mentioned family before. Other than his involvement with Carlos Navarra, he hadn't said anything about himself except his name. Various scenarios went through her mind. Broken home. Abusive family. Poor. Wealthy. Siblings or only child?

What if she initiated the conversation? Tell him about her family. Maybe he would open up to her. She had used this technique when interrogating suspects. Perhaps it would work with him. No, Erik would tell her about his past when he was ready and not a moment sooner.

About two hours later, Erik returned. She couldn't look at him without blushing. His face was red, too.

"You had quite the stack of mail, so I gave it a quick sort and brought what I thought was important back with me in the suitcase with your clothes." He bowed his head as he spoke and shifted awkwardly.

"Thanks. I'm sorry you had to do that for me."

"You're okay." His gaze went from the sink to the corner but never stayed on her for any length of time. "Oh, here's your key." Erik pulled the lanyard out of his pocket and placed it on the bed. "I best go. It's a long walk back to Onsite, and then I have to get to the methadone clinic."

"Will I see you tomorrow?" She remained hopeful he would agree. With any luck, by then, the embarrassment would have passed.

"Yes. I'll come as soon as I've had my treatment in the morning. We can spend the day together."

Hilary gave Xena a quick pat before her dog, and the man

left her hospital room.

If Erik returned the next day like he said he would, they needed something to do to pass the time. Before he went to her house to retrieve clothing for her, he had cleared it or said he had so she could leave the hospital. The lack of clothing held them back, but that excuse no longer existed.

Where could they go? The hospital was close to False Creek. Maybe he would take her along the paths that lined the shore. Granville Island? She'd not visited the Public Market in ages. Was that something which would interest Erik? It might be too girlie for him.

Thirteen

Onsite Detox Transitional Unit, East Hastings, Gastown, Vancouver

An uneasy feeling came over Erik that morning. The entire distance to the methadone clinic, he looked over his shoulder. Was he being followed? He thought so. His heart pounded, and he picked up his pace, eager to reach the safety of the medical centre. Xena bounded along beside him. When he walked in the front door, he was winded. Luck smiled down on him because the place was busy, and he had to wait in line for his treatment, allowing him to catch his breath.

Was this what being on the outside would be like? Continually watching for Navarra's thugs, never knowing when one of them might appear and life as he knew it would no longer be worth living? He hoped not. Still, he had to remain vigilant to prevent such a thing from occurring.

In his mind, it took forever for his turn to come, but he put it down to his anticipation of spending the day with Hilary.

After waiting for the prescribed length of time after receiving his methadone, Erik set out for Vancouver General in the most direct route possible.

Erik showed up at the hospital with Xena as promised. "Sorry, I'm so late. Everyone wanted to see Xena and fuss over her."

"She loved every minute of it, too, I'll bet."

"For sure. All the patients love her. Staff, too. You wouldn't believe how well behaved she was. Not hyper. If someone wanted to see her, we went into their room, and she sat and let them pet her. One little old lady cried. Said she was beautiful. I don't think she gets many visitors. She didn't want us to leave."

"Aw," Hilary said as she rubbed the top of her dog's head.

"So, where do you want to go?"

"What about Charleson Park and the paths along the water. They're not far from here. Granville Island is close, too."

"If you want." He snatched the blanket off the bed and laid it over Hilary's lap. "Don't want you getting a chill. Those in charge won't let you out again if you end up sick."

Hilary smiled, but inside, she knew he was right. Getting out of this place, even if just for a few hours and doing things that ordinary people did, had never been so important.

Out from under the shadow cast by the hospital building, Hilary tipped her face skyward. The sun's rays warmed her skin. Xena walked beside the wheelchair, keeping in line with the front wheel.

Erik pushed her chair down a slight grade on the tree-lined street. At the intersection of West Broadway stood the Speakeasy on one corner and the Pekoe Tea Lounge on another.

In the distance, skyscrapers stretched upwards. Their glass and concrete forms obliterated the majority of the view of the mountains beyond. Ominous clouds moved in, and the temperature dropped. The threat of rain was too real, and they were caught out without at least one umbrella or proper rain gear.

They continued walking in silence. Ideas of getting Erik to talk about himself swirled in Hilary's mind, but she didn't know how she could broach the subject, so kept quiet. No effort to talk on his part, so he must have been comfortable not speaking.

Too soon, they reached the end of Laurel Street. A wall of trees and a tall chainlink fence covered in vines prevented them from going further. The park was on the opposite side of the obstruction.

"We need to be up there." Hilary pointed to an overpass that stretched past the barricade.

"Oh," said Erik, his voice filled with resignation. "Hey, down there." He sounded perkier than before.

Before Hilary had a chance to react, he turned the wheelchair to the right, and they headed in that direction. They hadn't gone far when she saw what excited him — traffic lights. There was an intersection ahead with vehicles coming out from the direction they were unable to go in because of the fence.

Through a gap in the underbrush, a rail line appeared. That explained the need for the fence and a bridge. In no time, they reached the place where they could cross and continue their journey.

Erik pushed her chair through quiet residential streets, and eventually, they reached the shared walking-cycle path. In the distance, a lawnmower droned, and the sweet smell of freshly cut grass wafted on the breeze. The scent mingled with dried seaweed and gasoline from motorboats and water taxis moving across the water of False Creek.

At the fork in the paths, they took the one to the right, which ran along the shore. The iconic roof of BC Place peeked out between the high-rises. Soon the trail turned inland, and trees blocked the view of the water.

When they emerged, the clouds had dissipated, and the sun shone. Rhododendrons and other shrubs and trees lined the left side of the path. A figure stumbled out from the greenery and crashed into Hilary's wheelchair, and she screamed. Xena raised her hackles and growled at the person. Had Hilary been on active duty, she would have the man face down on the ground, her knee in the small of his back placing him in handcuffs. Instead, she was defenceless and vulnerable — two feelings foreign to her.

Erik helped the man to his feet. A bulbous nose took up most of his florid face and bushy eyebrows framed small, narrow-set hooded eyes. The stench of cheap liquor, halitosis, and body odour oozed from his pores. Thanks to her police training, she took in as many details of the man's appearance and physical state as she could before he scampered away.

One of the nearby trees had been taken over by a murder of crows. Their raucous calls filled the air. The cause of their agitation quickly became apparent. A Great Blue Heron perched in the top of an evergreen tree; its arrival so recent, its wings remained outstretched, attempting to maintain balance.

Something small landed on the sidewalk ahead of them with a crack followed by a single crow. The large, black shiny bird landed on the object and drove its beak into it repeatedly before picking it up and dropping it again.

Along the shoreline, more of the scavengers pounded on similar objects. One finally succeeded and cried out excitedly before gobbling the soft meaty centre — escargot in the Corvus world. Hilary preferred her snails steamed and served with lemon.

At the first bench away from trees and bushes, Erik stopped and parked Hilary's wheelchair before sitting next to her. Once the stranger was gone, Xena had stopped growling, and the hairs on her back returned to their normal position. The dog laid down and stretched out on her side on the grass.

After their unexpected encounter with the drunken vagrant, did she try to find out more about Erik? No. For now, lean back and enjoy the sun's warmth and the view. Calm down. Moored boats bobbed on the ripples. Sailboats made up the majority of the vessels, but a few yachts and other pleasure craft were on the water as well.

On the opposite shore, a patch of bright green glowed like a beacon. It was too bright to be grass. To the right stood the Cambie Street Bridge and to the left beyond a quay of floating docks, the Granville Bridge. A pair of mallards swam towards them but never came any closer than the rocky shoreline beyond the path.

"Why did you decide to become a cop?"

"My grandfather was on the force as was my father and a couple of uncles, too. Grandpa Dunbar received a commendation for bringing down a street gang."

Erik nodded. "Impressive."

"Okay, my turn now."

An expression Hilary couldn't read spread across his face.

"Why did you decide to get mixed up with heroin and become an addict?" she asked.

"Really? That's your question?" After a short pause, Erik continued. "I have no idea."

"You must have some inkling."

He scrubbed his palms on his thighs. "Homelife."

His body language told her he was uncomfortable talking about his previous life. If she pushed or asked him the wrong question, he would clam up. "You always lived in Vancouver?" That seemed a safe subject answered with a simple yes or no or the city he lived in before now.

"No. Grew up in Toronto."

Hilary had never been there, but the city appeared in the news frequently. She'd been to BC Place a couple of years ago for a football game when the Toronto Argonauts were in town. The force received tickets, and she went with some of the other off-duty cops.

"Any word when you'll get fitted for your new leg?"

That subject was not up for discussion. It meant the end of her days as a police officer. She turned away afraid if she didn't, she would start to cry.

"Sorry. Didn't mean to upset you." Erik reached out and touched her hand.

The gesture comforted her some, but it didn't bring back her missing limb. Nothing would do that.

"Maybe we should carry on," Erik said as he stood.

Xena jumped to her feet and wagged her tail.

"She's quite the character — has everyone at Onsite

fussing over her. At first, they weren't thrilled with her being there, but even Des has come round." Brakes released on the wheelchair, Erik turned it around, and they continued along the waterside path. "I call her my service dog. Your partner, whatshisname, is having his wife make her a vest, so it looks more official."

Service dog. It was apparent with her failure from the training program, police canine was not her calling. Maybe this would be better. Xena had a fantastic effect on Erik, and they seemed to like each other. If Kim were making the garment, she might bring it to the hospital. She didn't know the other woman well, but they had one thing in common — they were both women.

"The fitting is a couple of days away. My surgeon wanted to make sure all the swelling was gone first. I had a bit of infection and more bleeding than expected, which has slowed down the progress. They tell me the process will take about three weeks until I have a finished leg. Once I have that, I start physio and learn how to walk again. I will be so glad to get out of the hospital. The food sucks, and I'm bored senseless."

Hilary paused for a moment and scratched the stump of her leg. "You don't need to listen to me whine. Tell me more about you and growing up in Toronto."

"You don't want to hear about that. It's nothing special."

"I'll be the judge of that."

Erik wasn't going to win this battle with Hilary. He might as well get to it. The sooner he did, the sooner it would be over. "Okay. Grew up in Etobicoke on the west end of the city."

"I've heard of it."

"The old man worked at Goodyear until the plant closed. We lived in a dinky rented apartment on the top floor of a house on Islington Avenue. Some of the houses in the area were pretty shabby."

"After that?"

"He turned into a work-shy alcoholic. Picked up odd jobs here and there but drank away most of his earnings."

"Your mother?"

"She couldn't cope, so she spent most of her time in the bedroom reading romance novels."

"I'm sorry. I had no idea."

Erik's voice trembled, and he drew in a ragged breath. If she dropped the subject, he'd be much happier.

"Any brothers or sisters?"

"A sister. Older than me."

"Does she have a name?"

"Serenity."

"Married?"

"No idea, I started drinking when I was ten. Moved on to marijuana after that. When it didn't give me the escape I needed from my real world, I moved to harder drugs, and you know the rest." He stood and walked across the path towards the water.

She went too far with her continued prodding, but she wanted — no needed — to find out more about Erik. Hilary didn't blame him. By the sounds of things, his formative years were something he wanted to forget. They were something he had kept buried for a reason. She made a mess of things. "I'm sorry I upset you. All right?" She disengaged the brakes on the chair and wheeled across the path.

Erik placed his hands on the arms of her wheelchair, and looked her in the eye. "Now, you know. So, what's this fascination you have with Carlos Navarra? It's more than just me."

Tears welled up in her eyes. "My best friend growing up, Taylor Simpson, got mixed up with the creep. She died from one of his tainted batches of smack."

Erik stood and backed a few feet away. "So, you wanted me to roll on Navarra because of something that happened years ago." He smacked his forehead with the palm of his hand. "Not me at all, but your dead friend. You put my life at risk for something that happened in the past. I thought I knew you. Boy, did I have it wrong." He stormed down the path in the direction from which they came.

Hilary bashed the arms of her chair with her fists. Xena stood, cocked her head and took a few steps after Erik and looked back. She returned to Hilary's side, sat and rested her chin on her lap.

Was he right? Was she so desperate to avenge Taylor's death, she would use anyone to achieve her goal? She didn't intend to put Erik's life in danger any more than he had done himself, but she did. She mentally kicked herself in the backside for being so stupid and selfish. "Erik, wait. Come back. I'm sorry," she yelled, but it was too late. He was out of sight and well out of earshot.

Fourteen

Charleson Park, Vancouver

Hilary dashed tears away with one hand and struggled to pull her cellphone out of her pocket with the other. When she finally got hold of the device, she fumbled for a good grip, and her iPhone dropped to the ground in front of her chair. She tried moving the smartphone closer with her foot but pushed it farther away.

When she leaned forward, her fingers reached the case only to drop it again. The final stretch was disastrous. She toppled to the ground and pushed her wheelchair away in the process. The chair hit the curb and tipped over. She was too far from the bench to use its leverage to haul herself into an upright position.

Angry with herself for being so stupid and careless, she broke down and sobbed. Able to shift herself into a sitting position, she drew her knees to her chest and wrapped her arms around them. People walked by, but no one offered her any assistance. Their lack of compassion angered her more.

Luke. He would come and help her. She scanned the contact list until she found his cellphone number and dialled. "I need you," she blurted out as soon as he picked up.

"Hil, is that you?"

"Y-yes."

"Are you okay?"

She overheard Kim's voice and Luke telling her who he was with on the phone.

"N-no. Please. I need you."

"Where are you?"

"Charleson Park near the water."

"Stay put. On my way."

"No danger of me going anywhere."

"Gotta go. Hilary's in trouble."

Kim nodded. "Be careful," she said, her eyes welling up with tears.

Luke kissed her on the cheek, snatched the keys off the hook, and ran for the family minivan. Thankfully, he was off-duty when the distress call from his partner came. How did she go from the hospital to False Creek? Had one of Navarra's guys done this? He wouldn't put it past any of them. After all, Hilary recognized the tattoo on the back of the man's hand. He drove as fast as he could and as far into Charleson Park as possible before abandoning the vehicle and racing towards the water on foot.

The sight that greeted him broke his heart. Hilary was sitting in the middle of the path. Her wheelchair lay on its side next to the curb, Xena beside her. He scooped her into his arms and sat her on the bench, then retrieved her chair. "What happened? Are you okay? What happened?" he repeated his initial question, sitting beside her.

"Er-Erik brought me out."

"I told you that guy was trouble. Did he do this to you?"

"N-no. We fought, and he stormed off."

Luke wrapped his arm around her shoulders and pulled her close to him.

"I dropped my phone on the ground … and fell … fell out of the chair trying to reach it," she said between sobs. "My wheelchair rolled away and tipped over when the stupid thing hit the curb." She managed an entire sentence without breaking down.

How could he persuade her to tell him what she and Erik fought about that caused him to leave her abandoned in the park? "I'll look after you and take you back to the hospital, but first I need to know what happened. Can you tell me, please?"

Hilary drew in a ragged breath and stared through tear-filled eyes into his. "He thinks I'm morbidly obsessed with Carlos Navarra."

"Are you?"

"Yes. No. Kind of. But not like you think. I never told you this before. I haven't told anyone other than Erik and the sarge. My best friend going through high school, got mixed up with Navarra. She died after shooting up one of his noxious concoctions. Taylor, that was her name, can't stand up to Navarra now, so I'm trying to do the right thing. The creep deserves to be locked up. Anyway, Erik thinks I'm pressuring him to roll on the guy."

"And are you?" Luke shifted on the bench so he could look Hilary directly in the eye.

She squirmed. "Maybe. I want to see the scumbag go down for killing her and countless others. Erik is one of the few who survived."

"You ID'd Navarra from his tattoo. They caught the whole drug deal on security cameras. Won't that put him away?"

"It should, but I wanted eye-witness testimony to seal the deal. Ensure Navarra went down for the rest of his natural."

Of all the scenarios he played over in his mind racing to the park, this was the last thing Luke expected. Never, would he have guessed the enormity of the secret Hilary carried with her since her high school days. He didn't push her for more information on her friend or the circumstances surrounding her death. She told him. That was what mattered.

"Let's take you back to the hospital. We'll go from there." He helped her from the bench into her wheelchair and pushed her to where he left the minivan. Neither one spoke, but the silence between them was far from strained, unlike those last moments she was with Erik. Within ten minutes, Luke had

Hilary back in her hospital room.

Erik approached the Stamp's Landing Ferry Dock. That's when the recollection hit him. The drunken vagrant who shot out from the protected path was one of Carlos Navarra's guys. The man with the horrible breath who threatened him in the hospital that night. Did he abduct Hilary? Undoubtedly, Xena would have attacked him to protect her.

If anything happened to Hilary, he would never forgive himself. He shouldn't have gone off like that. Why did he leave her? It was unfair. Not taking any more time to ponder over the situation, he turned and raced back to where they stopped to rest and had argued. He needed to apologize.

The place where he left Hilary stood empty. He swore he returned to the right location — near the second pair of wooden benches arranged in a V and the path emerged from the woods.

Panic took over. His heart pounded to the point he thought it might explode. Beads of sweat formed on his forehead. His mouth dried, and he couldn't swallow. He clapped his hands on his head and paced in circles. The shrill ring of a bicycle bell made him pay attention to his surroundings, and he jumped out of the way just in time to avoid being run down.

Beyond the shrubs and flowers stood the seat where they rested. Children played in a nearby playground with swings, slides and monkey bars. Their squeals and laughter filled the air.

Here the curb was more of a seawall, so he crept to the water's edge to ensure he didn't find her lying facedown in the bay, drowned. No corpse. The ducks who swam towards them were nowhere in sight.

He dropped to the bench and put his face in his hands. He blew his chances with Hilary. The one good thing in his life and he ruined it. Did he report her missing? With no cellphone, he couldn't contact the police. Was there a payphone in the area? Even if there were, he would have to borrow money to place the call. Would the police take him seriously? Didn't you have to wait at least twenty-four hours before reporting a missing person?

Erik kicked at a few stones on the ground. The desire to pick one up and toss it as hard as he could into the water overwhelmed him. How could he be so stupid? First, his fight with Hilary and second, not recognizing the man straight away.

She was strong. Maybe she carried on along the paths further? He stood and continued. She couldn't have gone too far, even with the head start. When he found her, he'd get down on his knees and beg her forgiveness.

A young couple holding hands and walking a small dog approached.

Erik rushed to meet them. "Excuse me, did you happen to see a woman in a wheelchair with a German Shepherd?"

Both shook their heads and continued.

More people drew closer. He jogged to meet them. Breathless, he repeated his question. The answer was the same. No one had seen Hilary or Xena. His queries brought strange looks from many people, and their expressions worried him. What if someone reported him for harassment?

The path became more congested the longer he walked. A barricade indicating the entrance to the Spruce Harbour Marina prevented him from continuing in the same direction any further. The cycle path markings bypassed this private area, and he followed them. Townhouses and condos lined the left side of the walkway. Their neatly trimmed hedges offered some privacy from the walkers and cyclists. The only thing he was interested in finding was Hilary.

When he reached Granville Island, the number of people out and about made it impossible to see anything. If Hilary and Xena were in this crowd, they would be impossible to find. He jumped a few times to peer over the heads of the pedestrians who wandered like cattle. The pair had vanished.

Anxious for Hilary's wellbeing, he turned around and went back in the direction from which he came. By now, he feared to ask after her and Xena's whereabouts. An older couple walked down a side street near the marina. "Excuse me," he called and jogged up the narrow road towards them. "I'm wondering if you can help me. I'm looking for my friend. She's in a wheelchair and has her German Shepherd with her. Have you seen them?"

"Why yes," the woman answered. "Up at the end of this road by the no entry sign. There was a van parked there, and a man was helping her in. There was a big dog, too."

Van. Luke owned a minivan. He hoped the unknown man was him. Hilary could call him if she needed help. "Thank you so much," he said, taking the woman's hand in both his and shaking it.

Erik had to get to the hospital. He trotted off in what he thought was the right direction. After a few false starts, Erik found himself on the Laurel Street Land Bridge. He was almost there. Renewed, he jogged up the road.

In the doorway to Hilary's room, Erik skidded to a stop. She was safe. The burden since finding her missing when he returned to Charleson Park vanished. "Thank God, you're safe."

Luke turned and scowled at him. No, those dark eyes of his pierced through his heart.

"No thanks to you. Anything could have happened to her after you took off." He walked towards Erik pointing his finger at him before stabbing him in the chest with the outstretched digit. "Did you know she fell trying to pick up her phone after she dropped it?"

"N-no."

"If you didn't run off like you did, you would."

"Did she tell you why we argued?"

"Yes."

Hilary wheeled her chair over to where the men quarrelled. "Stop, you two. I'm sick of you being at each other's throats all the time. I want you both to leave."

Xena trotted to Hilary's side and sat.

"Fine, but before I go, here's something you didn't know about today. That drunken vagrant who stumbled out of the bushes was one of Navarra's guys. The one who threatened me when I was in intensive care. I'd recognize his 'something died inside' breath anywhere. I didn't realize at the time. Almost to the ferry docks when it hit me. I came back as soon as I realized, but you were gone. I thought he got you."

Hilary dropped her gaze to her lap. Luke rubbed the back of his neck with the hand he used earlier to back Erik into the wall.

"I'll call it in. Can you give me a description?"

Hilary went first. Luke recorded her details then turned to Erik. He couldn't add a thing. Her description was thorough. When they finished, Luke left the room, punching numbers on his cellphone as he walked.

"I'm sorry I bailed on you. You didn't deserve it."

"Hey, what's with the pity party?" A male hospital employee pushing a wheelchair strode to her side. "I'm here to take you for your fitting for your new leg."

Dressed in hospital green scrubs, nothing about his appearance stood out to her. He was one of the endless streams of medical care workers who came and went from her room.

The man set the brakes on the chair and helped her from where she sat into the seat, released them, and they were off. He whistled off-key as he walked. The sound grated on Hilary's nerves.

Downstairs, a patient transfer vehicle waited by the main doors. Hilary frowned. Was she going in that?

"Let's get you in," he said as he opened the door and lowered the wheelchair ramp.

"It's not done here at the hospital?"

"No. Don't worry. Vancouver Orthopaedic Group is only a few blocks away. They're the best. One of the guys designed Terry Fox's artificial leg. They've even made arms and legs and other things for the movies."

On their arrival at the clinic, an employee took Hilary into the back where they measured, photographed, weighed, and re-measured before they made the plaster cast of her stump. Now she played a waiting game while the specialists did their thing and created her new leg.

"The first prosthetic will be temporary. Give you a chance to grow used to walking with it. You'll start between parallel bars. It's a lot heavier than your natural leg."

"How long before?"

"A week. We've got all your measurements, so we'll get to work straight away."

By the time Hilary arrived back at Vancouver General, she was exhausted. If getting fit for a new limb was this tiring, how bad would walking be? She climbed on the bed and leaned back against the pillows. Her eyelids grew heavier, and in no time, she was asleep.

Fifteen

Vancouver General Hospital, West 12th Avenue, Vancouver

"Good afternoon, Dunbar," Sergeant Vincent said when he entered Hilary's room.

She spun her wheelchair around. Other than the grand Poobah and Luke, he was only the third member of the force to visit her. Was he going to tell her she could have her original job back?

He pulled over a chair and sat facing her.

Hilary couldn't read his facial expression. Even at roll call, he had one of those deadpan faces. "Hi. Nice to see you."

"Not sure how to break the news to you …"

"I'm not going back to active duty. The Chief Constable has already been in and laid things out. I take a desk job or public relations. Not going back on patrol."

"I wish I could've been the first to break the news to you. If I had my way, you would be back in that car with Stephanopoulos as soon as possible. Unfortunately, the orders come from above, and I have to abide by them — like it or not."

"I know. I sure as … don't. I'll tell you the same thing I told him. Shove it."

"Will you at least think about the offer?"

Hilary turned her wheelchair toward the bed, set the brakes and hoisted herself out and up onto the mattress. "I'm tired. I'm going to take a nap."

Sergeant Vincent stood and walked to the door. He paused with his hand on the frame. "Give it some thought … for me."

"Fine." She waved her hand, dismissing him from her room.

That afternoon, Erik arrived later than the usual time with Xena. She had proven to be quite the hit with the patients. On some of his visits, they took longer to reach Hilary's room because they visited longer with the others.

"Hey. Anyone from work been to visit you?"

"Is it that obvious?" She pushed the button and raised the head of her bed.

"What do you mean?" He lifted Xena to the mattress and pulled up a chair.

"Other than the grand Poobah the other day, Sergeant Vincent was in earlier. They're the only ones other than Luke, who've bothered to put in an appearance. And they both said the same thing. I won't be going back to active duty."

"Is that a bad thing?"

The daggers Hilary shot from her eyes burned into his chest. Dumb question on his part. "Okay, okay. Just askin'."

"I'm sorry. I shouldn't take things out on you. My choices are either desk job or public relations. Token wounded officer. Visit schools, carry a trophy into a sporting event if I've got a mind to."

"I can see where that wouldn't be challenging enough, but it would be safer. Less likelihood of you getting shot at those places."

"Don't be facetious."

"Sorry."

Hilary settled the dog on her lap and stroked her soft fur.

"Don't say anything — yet. Listen. Then you can tell me to get stuffed or whatever. Agree?"

She nodded.

"Because you were injured on the job, there's bound to be compensation from the province. Maybe additional compensation from the police. What happens to the police money if you decide to quit the force? Does that let them off the hook? If it dries up because you don't go back ..."

"Okay, I hear where you're coming from, but I don't want to do the mundane things they've pigeon-holed me into."

"What if? Hear me out. What if you went back and did those mundane things? Okay, you'd be the token trophy carrier, but you'd likely have a Monday to Friday job with no shift work. Consider it a re-entry point. Kinda like me at Onsite and my methadone program."

A frown appeared on her face, and she shook her head.

"In the meantime, go to the gym and work out until you're back in shape. Then, when you think the time is right, ask your superiors again about active duty."

"You seem to know an awful lot about this kind of stuff." Hilary swung around and dangled her leg and partial off the bed.

"You meet all kinds when you're on the streets," he said. "You're not a quitter. I can tell that."

"I'd have to pass a fitness test. It would be almost like going through the academy again."

Erik leaned forward and rested his hands on her thighs. "So? You can do it."

Xena changed positions and wormed her head under Erik's hand and rested her chin on her human. So far, Erik was the only person who visited regularly — but placing his hands on her legs? That was a bit too personal, even though they were warm and smooth. If she moved them, would he be offended? A chance she was willing to take. Hilary clutched his wrists and shifted his hands to the bed on either side of her.

"Sorry, got carried away," he mumbled as he got to his

feet and drifted to the window.

She did affront him. Swinging her legs over the footboard and shifting the dog, she spun around and faced him. "Sorry. I didn't mean to hurt your feelings. It's not you or anything you did; sometimes I wonder if people are polite and kind to me because I'm not whole anymore.

"People like that are shallow. They don't deserve your time. I hope you don't think I'm one of them."

"No ..." But did she?

"Come on, Xena. Time to go."

The dog jumped off the bed and sat at his side.

He clipped the leash to her collar and started for the door.

"Erik, please. Don't go," Hilary begged. "I'm sorry. I made a mess of things. You're not shallow. You're far from it. You've been a true friend to me since the accident."

By the time she finished talking, he and the puppy were gone.

Sixteen

Vancouver General Hospital, West 12th Avenue, Vancouver

Hilary's surgeon stopped in on his rounds. He rechecked her leg. Pleased with the surgical site's appearance, he signed off on the form. "You're free to leave any time you're ready."

"Thank you. I have to arrange transport now that I know for sure I'm leaving here today."

"Take your time. I'm off to enter your release into the computer."

The man disappeared from her room. Going home. Those two words were music to her ears. She couldn't leave soon enough. Cellphone clutched in one hand, she hobbled to the window and punched in Luke's number. It went to voicemail. Disappointed, she made a start gathering her belongings. Since Erik brought her clothes from home, she had a suitcase and not just the large green garbage bag the nurse gave her when she changed rooms.

A pair of crutches stood in the corner by the closet. Hilary scowled at them as she pulled her luggage from the locker. She barely used them during her entire hospitalization. The wheelchair was her mode of conveyance to go anywhere other than her room before having her prosthetic fitted. Within her private accommodations, which were cramped, she managed without any assistance: chair or hop. After receiving her artificial leg, she walked in the corridor holding the handrail affixed to the wall.

Erik needed to know, too, so he could bring Xena to her house. She dialled the number for Onsite. When a woman's voice answered the phone, she said, "Can I speak to Erik Layne, please?"

Heavy footsteps clomped through the phone. Then the person yelled Erik's name at the top of her lungs. Hilary was forced to move her cellphone away from her ear; the noise was so loud and harsh.

More footfalls. This person was running. "Erik speaking," he said breathlessly.

"It's Hilary. I'm free. They've sprung me." Not giving him a chance to get a word in, she continued. "I'm going home."

"When? I mean, what time?"

"As soon as I can arrange a ride. You can bring Xena home around one. I should be there by then."

"Great."

The disappointment in his voice was evident. Hilary hated hurting him by asking for Xena to come home, but the dog was hers. Erik was welcome to come and visit anytime, and she would be sure to tell him that when he brought Xena.

With Luke's number punched into her phone, Hilary waited as it rang, hoping he picked up this time. "Stephanopoulos here."

She sighed with relief. "Hi, Luke. It's Hilary. I need a favour."

"What's up?"

"They've released me from the hospital."

"Wonderful."

"I need a ride home. Can you do it?"

"I'm on duty. Can you wait for my break? I'll come then.

See you about ten-thirty, okay?"

"Sure." Although disappointed, she understood Luke couldn't drop everything for her. His job came first. If she was still on patrol with him and it was Kim who phoned, she would have to wait for the timing to be right.

The morning crept by slowly. Members of the hospital staff stopped by and said their goodbyes. Hilary's hospitalization lasted so long; it was like saying goodbye to family members.

Finally, Luke appeared in her doorway. She was about to walk down the corridor to the elevators when Pat squashed her plan.

"Sorry, hon. Hospital policy. You need to ride out of here in a wheelchair. Once you're outside the door, you're free to do as you please, but in here, you get to sit in one of our luxury chairs on wheels and let someone propel you to freedom." The woman laughed. "Your carriage awaits," she finished.

Hilary's mood lifted, and she took a seat. Luke walked beside her, trundling her suitcase, and Pat brought up the rear, pushing the method of transport.

Luke left the cruiser in one of the police parking bays near the emergency entrance. Still, he managed to steer everyone in that general direction before they exited the building. Yes, Hilary might have a prosthetic leg now, but he didn't want her walking any further than necessary.

"Where's Rodriguez?" she asked, her hand resting on the door handle.

"Dropped him at the station. Glad of the downtime from him. He tires me out," he said, placing Hilary's suitcase in the trunk of the car. Luke walked to the passenger side of the vehicle, cane in hand, and pulled open the door for Hilary.

She supported her weight with the walking stick, lifted her left leg to climb in but stopped. Foot back on the ground; she repeated the process. This time her foot reached the floor mat. Still, she couldn't get herself into the car.

Did he let her try a few more times on her own or help her

straight away? He couldn't bear to watch his ex-partner struggle any longer, so he went to her aid. Within minutes, he had her settled on the front seat. The simple act of getting into a car thwarted her. It bothered him to see her in such a predicament.

Luke circled the car. He needed a moment to pull himself together before climbing into the driver's seat. A couple of deep breaths and he opened the door and eased in behind the wheel. What would he be like at her house if he was this much of a basket case now? Stairs to climb to reach the front door. More stairs to the upper floor.

About ten minutes after leaving Vancouver General, Luke pulled the police car to a stop opposite Hilary's house. She clambered out. Was it more comfortable for her because it was her natural leg she exited with or was it her joy of being home? Whatever the reason, he was happy to see she could move around freely. He kicked himself for not spending more time at the hospital visiting her. He knew two of their superiors had been in to see her. No one from their shift or the opposite ones took the time.

To say she didn't have her new prosthetic for long, Hilary navigated rather well on it. She had a bit of an awkward gait, but he assumed in time that would disappear. By now, she stood at the foot of the stairs leading to her front door. The cane he provided for her tucked under her arm. He hurried around the car and retrieved her bag.

The pink lanyard with the purple hippo dangled from the deadbolt. Hilary was quick. He had no further doubt that she was pleased to be back home.

Erik put Xena in the backseat of Des's Toyota then loaded all the dog's things into the trunk. "Appreciate you doing this for me. A bit far when you have to carry all that."

"No problem. Maybe now, without the mutt, things will return to normal here. Not that the dog was a pain, but we have a routine, and having her interrupted it."

The men climbed into the car, and Des pulled away from

the curb. At the traffic lights at Main Street, he turned right. Xena sat in the middle of the backseat, with her head between the seats.

"You're sure your lady friend gets out today?"

"Yup." Erik stole a glance at the dashboard clock. "Should be there by now."

They passed under the glassed-in walkway for the Expo line, near the train and bus stations. Off to the right, the dome of the Science Centre glowed in the sun. This part of the city was new to Erik, and he turned his head from side to side, taking in his surroundings. On his walks to visit Hilary in the hospital, he passed by BC Place by way of Pacific Boulevard — the opposite side of False Creek.

After Des turned off the primary thoroughfare, they passed through a section of commercial and residential units. Soon they were in a quiet neighbourhood. Small houses and apartments lined the right side of the street and a school with an enormous playground sprawled down the other. A right turn at a small roundabout brought them to yet another unrecognizable road. Not until they reached the soccer field on the right, did anything look familiar.

Des brought the car to a stop across from Hilary's house. Xena pranced and whined in the backseat. Her behaviour said she knew she was home.

"Not until I get your leash clipped on you," said Erik as he eased out of the front seat and opened the back door. He grabbed the dog's collar and snapped the lead to it. "Come on then, girl. Let's go."

As he walked her across the street, a melancholy feeling came over him. Not only would it be strange and lonely without Xena, but would Hilary want to have anything to do with him now he was no longer looking after the dog?

Des unloaded the trunk of the car while he walked across the street with his canine companion.

By the time Erik and Xena reached the top step, Hilary held the front door open. He unsnapped the leash, and the dog raced into the house, knocking Hilary off balance. Erik reached out and steadied her to keep her from falling. For a few moments, their eyes locked on one another's. They might have remained that way longer, but were interrupted by Des and the first load of the dog's things.

Erik released his grasp on Hilary and trotted across the street to collect the rest of it. Something happened in that moment when they gazed at each other, and having Des around made it impossible to find out exactly what it was.

"I just made a pot of coffee. Do you want to stay for a cup?"

"No, I better head back. Thanks, though." Des sat the bag of food and dishes on the floor inside the front door and backed away.

Erik heaved a sigh, which drew a stare from Hilary. He didn't think it came out so loud. "Sure, would love one." Anything to spend more time with her.

Hilary returned to the kitchen. The last thing she wanted was people in her house, but they brought Xena home, so the least she could do was make an effort. Since Des declined her offer, only Erik remained, and he'd leave when she asked.

"Sorry, no cream," she apologized. "Not that it would be fit for human consumption anyway." She rooted in the cupboard above her Keurig and withdrew a container of Coffeemate. "At least this stuff doesn't curdle."

Sugar bowl, mugs with hand-painted German Shepherd puppies on them, and spoons out, Hilary poured them each a cup of Colombian from the thermal carafe. When she bought the new coffeemaker, she chose this one because of its practicality. Most times, she only wanted a mug, but if she had visitors, she could make a pot at a time.

Holding her cup in both hands, she brought the steaming medium roast to her lips and sipped. "Mmm. This blend is delicious. I've been waiting for this moment since I woke up in the hospital. That slop they pass off as coffee is disgusting."

"Agreed."

Xena padded through the room and scratched at the back door. Hilary let her out and went back to Erik.

"I'm so glad I'm out of there and back home with my things, and my dog. Not being checked on by every member of the medical staff each time they passed my room. I honestly think they figured I'd hang myself from the blinds." She swallowed another mouthful of coffee.

A bark resounded through the small room, and this time Erik tended to the dog.

Having a man around had its advantages. He could look after the yard work, putting out the trash and recycling, and bringing in the empty containers.

The one standing in her kitchen would do anything for her. The only thing Erik couldn't do was turn back the clock to before the shooting and make her whole again.

"Hey, what time is it?" he asked.

Hilary pointed to the digital clock on the stove.

"I better go. By the time I walk back to Gastown, it will be time to go for my methadone treatment." Erik placed his mug in the sink and turned to the front door.

Tears burnt Hilary's eyes, but she blinked them back. His sudden change in attitude took her by surprise. One minute they were chatting and enjoying the other's company and the next, he couldn't take off fast enough.

"You need anything before I go?"

"No, you're fine. I'm going to lie down for a while. I'm wiped out."

Hilary followed and and leaned against the door when it closed and latched behind her. The tears now flowed. She loped into the living room, threw herself on the couch and sobbed.

Xena padded to the couch, sat and rested her chin on the sofa in front of Hilary's face.

Two days passed with no sign of Erik. He bailed on her at the first opportunity. Who wanted someone like her? Someone who was no longer whole. Even though the thought lingered in the back of her mind, she'd hoped he was different. He wasn't. He *was* shallow.

Since coming home from the hospital, Hilary hadn't attempted the stairs, even though she had a cane to help her and a sturdy railing to hold. She had a powder room downstairs, so made do with it. The sofa doubled as her bed: the coffee table, her medicine chest. Her multitude of medications lined up like soldiers on its surface — antidepressants, antipsychotics, antibiotics and a host of others, anti or otherwise.

Seventeen

Luke's House, East 22nd Avenue, Vancouver

"Leah, Emma, I'm not telling you again. It's time we were leaving," Kim called down the hall towards their bedroom.

"Want me to try?" Luke offered.

"Please do. Some days trying to get those two ready to go anywhere is like herding cats — and we all know how well that works."

He chuckled and disappeared down the corridor. Shrieks of laughter emanated from the back of the house. Minutes later, Luke emerged carrying a wriggling child under each arm.

"Why don't you call Hilary and invite her to come with us?"

"Great idea. You three head to the van and I'll be out shortly."

Kim grabbed her purse and put the strap of the crossbody bag over her shoulder. Daughter on either side of her, the three went out the back door.

Luke punched Hilary's number into his cellphone. It rang out without her answering, so he tried again. This time after five rings, the call was disconnected. She hung up. The process went on repeatedly as he walked through the house, ensuring it was secure, and the burners on the gas stove were off.

When he reached the van, he said, "Hilary's not picking up."

"Maybe she had an appointment?"

"She's home. She keeps hanging up on me. I'm worried. Do you still have the spare key to her house? The one she gave me when she first got the dog?"

"Um, I think so. Should be on my keychain." Kim rummaged in her oversized bag and came out with a dolphin-shaped ring with several keys hanging from it.

"We're going over there," he said. Ice water coursed through his veins, making the hairs on the back of his neck and arms stand on end, like goosebumps, but not caused by being cold. Fear was the cause. What if Hilary did something stupid? What if that was the reason she kept putting him on ignore?

"You don't think …"

He raked his hand through his hair and snapped, "Right now, I don't know what to think."

Kim scrambled into the passenger seat while Luke circled the van. "Girls buckled in?" he asked, sliding behind the wheel. He turned the key, but the minivan didn't start. The starter made a sickly groaning sound. "AAARGH! This piece of …" He whacked the steering wheel with the heel of his hand.

"Not in front of the girls."

Luke gulped down a deep breath and exhaled slowly then tried the key in the ignition again. This time the engine started. When he turned from their driveway on to the street, the tires squealed. The girls giggled.

Typically, the drive from his place to Hilary's took about ten minutes. He brought the van to a screeching halt in front of her house in less than that. The drawn curtains kept the house in darkness — no indication of any lamps being on.

"Stay here," he instructed as he leapt out of the vehicle, leaving the door wide open, and raced up the front steps. The small front yard, which was usually neatly manicured, stood neglected. Chicory and dandelions gone to seed had taken over the grass. In the border of the flower bed, a Scotch thistle stood about eighteen inches tall.

His hands shook as he tried to put the key in the Yale lock. After several unsuccessful attempts, he gained entry.

Hilary sat on the sofa. She didn't acknowledge his presence when he barged in. Xena looked up from her bed then put her head back down again. Luke took a few steps into the living room. Tears ran down his former partner's cheeks. She had a book or something in her lap, so he moved closer.

She held the remnants of a photo she ripped up in her hands. A few pieces dropped to the album. They were academy graduation pictures. Another photo of Hilary as a teenager and another girl, presumably Taylor, hamming it up for the unknown photographer, remained in pristine condition.

A basket on the coffee table held several prescription bottles. Luke picked them up one by one. "You haven't taken any of these, have you?"

She shook her head.

"I came to see what's taking so long," Kim said.

"I thought I told you to stay in the van."

"Xena," Emma cried.

The dog jumped from her bed and lavished the little girl with kisses. Leah joined her. Great, now he had the whole family with him — not how he envisioned it would play out.

"Let me talk to her. You and the girls take the dog over to the park at the end of the street. I'll call you when I want you to come back."

If anyone could reason with Hilary in this state, his wife could. Kim had that way about her. "Okay, come on, girls. Let's do what your mother said."

Kim waited for the house to quiet before opening the curtains. "There, much better. Not so dark." A layer of dust covered the hard furnishings. With the drapes closed, the dirt didn't show. She sat beside Hilary and put a loving arm around her shoulders. "Penny for them."

"I'm, I'm just so tired," she whispered, looking at Kim

through red, tear-filled eyes. "If only I could turn back the clock. Go back to before the shooting."

"Unfortunately, that's impossible." Kim plucked a tissue from the box on the end table and dried Hilary's eyes. "Lukas told me some things. Is that you and your friend?" She pointed to the photograph.

Hilary nodded. "On our hiking trip to the Whistler Train Wreck. We were sixteen at the time and boy crazy."

"And would your friend want you to spend your time holed up in your house like a hermit? You look like you were enjoying yourselves there."

"We, we were."

"We're taking the girls to the Vancouver Lookout. I suggested you come with us."

"No, thanks."

"You'd rather sit here in the dark and mope. Well, not today. You're coming with us, and you're going to enjoy yourself."

Hilary answered by rolling her eyes.

Why had Luke and his family turned up unannounced like this? Hilary didn't want visitors. She wanted things to be just as they were. Since the last time she saw Erik, being alone and miserable became the norm. Why hadn't he at least phoned her? Was she so repulsive to him that speaking to her revolted him? Being in her company, she could understand.

By now, Kim had her by the elbow and was lifting her from the couch. Hilary shook her off and dropped to the cushions sending a cloud of dust exploding into the air like ash from an erupting volcano. "I said I didn't want to go."

"Quit being such a misery guts. The fresh air and sunshine will do you good. Besides, you'll be with Lukas, the girls and me. Do you think we'd let anything happen to you?" Not giving the woman a chance to comment, Kim continued, "Of course, not."

Luke's wife reached out to retake Hilary's arm and was brushed off. Hilary stood without assistance. "You're not going to give me a minute's peace until I say I'll go with you. All right, I'll go, but I'm not leaving the house looking like this."

Kim followed Hilary towards the downstairs powder room. She stopped in the kitchen. Dirty dishes, primarily coffee cups and glasses, filled the sink.

A musty scent mingled with the fetidness of decaying meat. The garbage can? No. New bag. The oven? It, too, was empty. Where did the awful stink originate? The fridge? Kim opened the door. A few bottles of salad dressing, jars of mayonnaise and jam, but no fresh food no longer fit to eat.

The only appliance she had not checked was the dishwasher. When she opened the door, the pungent stench overpowered her. Had Hilary not run the thing since before her accident? Sounded logical. The woman was in the hospital until recently. She probably went off to work in the morning with the idea of running it that night; only she never came home.

"Where do you keep your dishwasher detergent?" Kim asked.

"Cupboard under the sink. A tub of pods."

Armed with two of the soap capsules, she opened the dishwasher, loaded them into the dispenser and quickly closed the door. Kim punched extra dirty, followed by the sanitize setting and started the machine. The place might stink for a while because of the hot steam venting out, but the odour wouldn't last forever. By the time she and her family brought Hilary home, it would have dissipated. For added insurance, she cracked open the window over the sink.

Twenty minutes later, Hilary emerged dressed in boot-cut jeans and a black sweatshirt. Still uncertain about going out, sweat dampened the back of her neck and her armpits. Was she making a mistake? It was too late; she'd agreed to the trip to the Lookout with Luke and his entourage and backing out now would send up red flags. No, go along with them, and get it over. The sooner they got there, and to the top, the sooner she'd be back home with Xena. On her way out the front door, Hilary grabbed her cane.

The van was higher off the ground than the police cruiser. Would she even be able to climb into it? She struggled to enter the force's vehicle.

Luke, the girls, and Xena walked towards them. Hilary glanced over her shoulder. Kim was waving her left arm above her head. The trio and dog drew next to the minivan, and Kim opened the door. The girls scrambled into the back seat. "I'll sit back here with them. It will be easier for you in the front."

Hilary nodded; her eyes fixed on her dog and Luke as he led her into the house. When he returned to the van, he helped Hilary into the passenger seat, then strode around and climbed in behind the wheel.

Soon they were driving down Quebec Street. Vancouver had transformed into one gigantic construction zone, slowing their progress. Hilary stared out the window at the passing scenery. Many of the streets, she and Luke patrolled when they were on-duty. After a right turn on to Seymour Street, he pulled the van to the curb. "I'll let you guys out here and go park. Meet you inside in a few." He hopped out and helped the other occupants before driving to the intersection and disappearing around the corner.

Up the hill from the lookout, the Seymour Building, with its distinct white lettering on a black background, was dwarfed by the newer Scotiabank tower behind it. She and Luke patrolled this area often. West Cordova Street, East Hastings, Water Street, Seymour Street and more. In the opposite direction stood Waterfront Station, once the central railway hub for the city. Now it was the terminus for the Skytrain system, SeaBus, and the West Coast Express. When she tipped her head back, only a sliver of the round observation deck, many storeys up, was visible.

Inside the doors, a ramp was available off to the side for those who required it. Hilary could navigate reasonably well on a flat surface, but steps proved troublesome at times. She opted for the sloped surface. In all the years she lived in the city, she never once went to the top of the Vancouver Lookout.

Luke soon joined them inside, and after paying the fare, they boarded the glass elevator for the ascent to the top. As it rose, the view changed dramatically. The Seymour Building was lower than them. A clock tower peeked out from behind other structures. The Cathedral of Our Lady of the Holy Rosary took pride of place unobstructed from view by the buildings around it.

From street level, trees and buildings were the only things visible. Glass ones, stone ones, brick ones. Maybe an occasional glimpse of the harbour from one of the streets dead-ending at the rail line. From the top of the lookout, the snowcapped mountains behind North Vancouver became visible. The area had so much beauty, yet it was invisible unless you were above the concrete jungle. The sun glinted off the snow, making it sparkle.

A cruise ship stood anchored at the pier in front of Canada Place. The building's iconic roof resembled the sails from vessels long ago. Ocean-going freighters queued for berths at the various freight docks. The West Coast Express commuter train lined the three tracks closest to the station building, and freight cars, mostly tankers and hoppers, occupied the other rails. Diesel engines shunted them to and fro, creating complete trains.

The cenotaph in Victory Park normally stood head and shoulders above the surrounding trees and lampposts. The shades on the lights were designed to resemble army helmets. Now, the trees and other surroundings dwarfed it. The Dominion Building, located across the street from the green space, was once the tallest in Vancouver. Its claim to fame only lasted two years before The Sun Tower usurped it. It was strange to see the building and the rest of the city from this angle.

Luke and Kim had to carry the girls so they could see since the windows were higher than they were tall. Hilary took her time inspecting her surroundings. She wouldn't admit it to anyone, but she was enjoying being out and seeing the city from a different viewpoint.

In the distance, a collection of high rises huddled together reached skywards like a cluster of basalt columns reminiscent of the Giant's Causeway in Northern Ireland and Fingal's Cave in Scotland. Hilary had never been to either country, so why she made the connection baffled her.

As she wandered leisurely, Rogers Arena and BC Place came into view. Behind them, False Creek. A memorial to the runner, Terry Fox, stood in front of the football stadium. Invisible from this angle, Hilary had seen it many times before her accident. This kid attempted to run, on an artificial leg, across Canada to raise money for cancer research — the cause of him losing his limb.

Fox made his run before Hilary's birth, but here she was lamenting the fact she lost her leg in a shooting, rather than getting out and doing something positive.

After making a complete circuit, exhaustion struck. The high tables and bar stools were a welcome sight. Hilary sat on one of the seats. It was a relief to get off her feet — correction, foot.

Luke, Kim, and the girls would have to pass by this area to return to the elevators. Within moments, Leah and Emma charged around the corner without their parents. While neither child was overweight, carrying them for any length of time would test a person's stamina. They likely became too heavy and were let down for respite.

Soon after, Luke's children raced past, a little boy about the same age as Emma, judging by his size, wearing navy shorts and matching hoodie, a white T-shirt, and Nike running shoes, rushed past. What immediately struck Hilary was he had an artificial leg.

Here was a small child, not letting his disability slow him down. All Hilary had done since waking up after surgery to discover the surgeons had taken her leg was moan and feel sorry for herself. She put on a brave front at times, but deep inside; she wallowed in self-pity. The uncertainty of returning to work played on her mind, too. She desperately wanted to go back to active duty. Her superiors were against that. Until that day, she never considered herself a defeatist, but now she wasn't so sure.

Luke and Kim rounded the corner, each holding one of the girls' hands. That same little boy followed. He approached Hilary and looked up at her with bright, blue eyes then squatted and lifted her pant leg. "Like me," he exclaimed.

At that instant, a harried woman shrieked, "Rory Mackie, you stop that instantly." She rushed over to Hilary's side and snatched the child away, her face crimson with embarrassment. "I don't know what to say."

The mother marched him over near the windows away from the seating area and reprimanded him.

He pointed to his artificial limb. "But, mommy, she's like me."

Exasperation took over, and she threw her hands in the air. Rory took advantage and ran back to the table where Hilary sat.

"I think your mother is upset with you," she said.

The child dropped his chin against his chest. Great, now the kid's mother would be after Hilary. In an attempt to diffuse the situation before it blew out of proportion, she raised the leg of her jeans so he could have a better look.

"I am so-so sorry," the woman babbled. "I don't know what got into him. He's not like this. Hey, you're the police officer who was shot."

Hilary envisioned the cogs and gears turn as Rory's mother put together the situation. "How did your son lose his leg?"

"Lawn tractor. He was riding on it with his dad and fell off. The mower ran over him."

"I see it doesn't slow him down any." Hilary smiled at the woman. The father's guilt after the accident had to be overwhelming. Riding lawnmowers were meant for one person and one person only — the driver.

Mrs. Mackie forced a smile in return.

One look at the woman and Hilary knew the accident affected her badly, too.

"Seen enough for one day," Luke asked, interrupting their conversation. Leah tugged on his arm.

Rory's mother took his hand, and they started for the

elevator. He looked back over his shoulder and waved. Hilary raised hers and bade him farewell.

Suddenly, Hilary's shoulders felt like a huge weight had lifted from them, but there was one more thing she had to do before Luke drove her home. "Yes, but can we stop by the Terry Fox Memorial at BC Place on the way home?"

"Well, there's not a lot of parking around there."

Kim slapped his arm.

"Sure. I can always drop you there, drive around the block until you're ready, then pick you up."

Once everyone was in the van, they set out. Right turns followed by lefts, finishing with two more rights. Luke brought the vehicle to a stop at the curb behind the last parking spot on Robson. "We'll wait here for you. Don't be too long. It wouldn't look good for an off-duty cop to receive a traffic ticket."

"Luke," Kim scolded then turned to Hilary. "You take as long as you need. We'll wait for you."

He wouldn't win this battle. The two women had ganged up on him big time. Oh well. If it meant Hilary getting back to her old self, then who was he to argue?

Luke adjusted the rear-view mirror so he could watch her. The woman was strong-minded, and her determination would get her through this. Eventually. The light changed, and Hilary crossed the street.

"Think she'll be okay?"

"Yes. Now stop worrying."

Gaze returned to the mirror, Luke kept a close watch on his partner.

Hilary walked up to the statue closest to the street, which was also the largest of the four. The image on the big screen mounted on the wall of the stadium changed.

She remained stalk still as the video played until it reached the spot where she started watching. Then she returned her attention to the next statue in line — this one slightly smaller.

I don't know how you felt when you first found out your leg would have to be amputated. But you turned your life around and made something of yourself. We lost our limbs for different reasons. Yours to cancer. Mine to a bullet. Had you come to terms with your disease by the time they took your leg? I didn't have that luxury.

One minute I had both of mine. The next, I'm waking up in the hospital to find out my lower leg is in the medical waste. There had to be something you held on to, kept you going. Something that prevented you from crawling inside yourself and giving up. You're far stronger than I am or will ever be. I wish I could have known you.

I met a little boy today. He lost his lower leg in a lawnmower accident. He didn't let it slow him down one bit. I'm guessing that because I didn't know him before the mishap. If he can do it, then so can I.

A tear escaped and dripped on her cheek, and she dashed it away. She was tired of crying. Tired of feeling sorry for herself. Just plain tired.

Back on the big screen, Terry loped along the side of the road in his quest to raise money for cancer research. She turned back to the series of statues. They emulated his hop, skip, run stride.

Hilary sucked in a deep breath. *I promise to be a better person and not let my disability get the better of me.*

Warmth and happiness washed over her. No longer would she mope around and feel sorry for herself. Those days were over. She walked away from the memorial, having accomplished what she came here for. It was up to her now.

Hilary refused Luke's help when he pulled the van up in front of her house. This was the first day of the new, confident Hilary. More like the one she was in the past when she graduated from the police academy and joined the ranks of the Vancouver force.

While her movement was ungainly, she darted, as best she

could, across the street and up her front steps. Xena barked at the sound of the key scraping its way into the Yale deadbolt.

Once inside, Hilary sidestepped her happy hound and entered the living room. The room needed a good clean. She picked up the basket of prescriptions and took it to the kitchen. After depositing it on the counter, she pulled out her Swiffer duster, a can of furniture polish, and a microfibre cloth.

Hard furnishings gleaming, she moved on to the soft ones. Xena went crazy when the vacuum cleaner was turned on. She barked and attacked it. Hilary finally locked her in the kitchen and closed the baby gate she installed soon after bringing the dog home, except back then it was to keep her out of the room.

Hours later, everything in the entire house had been cleaned, dusted, and vacuumed. The windows opened, and the house received a good airing. Dishwasher unloaded, and the dirty dishes from the sink loaded and running again. Xena freed from her prison. Exhausted, Hilary dropped on the sofa. The German Shepherd plopped on the floor and rested her chin on Hilary's thigh.

Hilary's eyes grew heavy, and her head bowed. She jerked herself awake. Seven o'clock was too early to fall asleep. After working herself out from under her dog's head, she padded to the kitchen. Once she fed Xena, Hilary ordered a che figata, with fresh garlic, pizza from a nearby pizzeria.

While she waited for its delivery, she hunted for something to drink with it. Her usual go-to when eating pizza was milk, but she didn't have any. In one of her lower cabinets, she found a case of cola and put a can in the fridge.

About forty minutes after placing the call, the doorbell rang. Xena was again banished to the kitchen. The savoury aromas escaping from the pizza box made Hilary's mouth water. She paid the delivery person and gave him a generous tip before heading to her kitchen.

After she opened the cardboard carton, Hilary leaned over and inhaled the mix of scents. The spicy chorizo, pungent garlic, sweet mozzarella, and the savoury-sweet caramelized onions. When she pulled a piece away, the cheese stretched, and she had to pinch it off between her thumb and forefinger to separate it from the rest of the delicious offering.

Thanks to the delicious smells and the fact she was ravenous, Hilary devoured the first piece in no time. All the hard work cleaning the long-since neglected house worked up her appetite. Soon into the second, she pulled the drink out of the fridge and poured it into a tumbler and topped it with frost-covered ice cubes.

Partway through the third, she conceded and put it back in the box and stuffed the leftovers in the oven. She would have cold pizza for breakfast.

Eleven o'clock came and rather than sleep on the sofa as had been the norm, Hilary climbed the steps and crawled into her warm, comfortable bed. As she snuggled under the duvet, Xena jumped and curled up beside her.

The following morning, pounding on the front door roused Hilary from her sleep. Xena charged down the stairs barking. She swung her legs off the bed and pulled on her prosthetic. Thanks to a small porch roof over the entryway, a cursory glance out the bedroom window revealed nothing. She tugged on a pair of sweatpants and yanked the pullover she wore the previous day over her head before heading downstairs.

The silhouette of a person's body was visible through the front door's window. With the way the dog barked and snarled, she didn't dare open it. Anyone could be out there, including Navarra or one of his thugs.

"Xena, stop," she ordered, but it was to no avail. The animal persisted.

The mail flap creaked open. Someone was going to kill her. In her panic, Hilary thought the barrel of a gun protruded from the narrow opening. Her heart raced as she looked around for a weapon she could use to defend herself and her dog. Nothing.

"You can stop now, Xena. It's me. Use your inside voice, girl," the man outside the door said.

Erik! Hilary unlatched the deadbolt and pulled open the door. "You frightened the life out of me."

"Sorry. You going to let me in or do I have to stay out here?"

"Where have you been?"

"Tied up at Onsite. Things I needed to do and couldn't when I was looking after Xena."

It might have been a lie, but his eyes said he told the truth. Hilary moved aside.

Erik stepped into the front hall. The raised cover of the roll-top desk in the living room exposed an open laptop computer on the work surface. He could find out about his family.

Hilary paused by the door. "You coming?"

"Yeah. I didn't know you had a computer."

"Do you want to use it?"

"If you don't mind. Would kinda like to find out about my family."

"Sure, no problem."

Hilary walked ahead of him. Her gait was awkward because of her prosthetic, but the longer she walked, the more natural it became. It was as if it seized up if she didn't move frequently.

In the living room, she sat on the arm of the couch. She pointed to the chair in front of the desk. "You sit there."

Erik stared at the screen. He didn't have a clue how to use a computer. More regrets. With his lack of qualifications, he'd never find work — at least not decent work. Washing dishes was about all he was qualified for, and that might require a high school diploma. He made a mental note to talk about it to Des when he returned. How did he ask for Hilary's help with the computer and not sound like a total idiot? He took a deep breath and said, "I'm sorry, never used a computer before. Would you help me."

"Absolutely."

Hilary clicked the buttons on the mouse and brought up

her favourite browser, Chrome.

Xena squeezed in between them. Hilary patted the dog on the head. "What do you want to search for? As they say, the world is your oyster."

"Can we try to find my parents?"

"Sure. Type their names in the search bar."

With one finger, Erik hunted and pecked his way around the keyboard. Using a computer was something she took for granted, but here was someone who had never used one and couldn't type. His talents lie elsewhere. Xena was a completely different animal now since spending time with Erik. Other than the initial excitement of being home, she didn't charge from one room to another noisily. Now the dog was laid back and calm. Okay, she still wanted to be the centre of attention, which was evident with the way she wormed her way in between them.

Erik had finally typed the 'e' at the end of his surname.

"Hit the enter key," she said and pointed to its location on the keyboard.

He did. The computer chewed on the data and presented them with a long list of people and street names. Some results might even have been villages.

Hilary leaned over from her place on the arm of the sofa. "Let me drive, and we'll get you started."

Erik stood. "Here, you take this chair. I'll grab another one."

Seated side by side on two chairs in front of the desk and computer screen, she took over.

"No use. We'll never find them," Erik moaned. "It was a dumb idea."

"Not dumb by any means. We just have to narrow the search. You said you grew up in Etobicoke. Let's try your surname and that." Hilary's fingers flew over the keys. "Ready?"

Erik held his breath, unsure of what, if anything, they would find. Better yet, did he want to see the results of their search? It wasn't like he left home on the best of terms.

"Right there." He aimed his index finger at the screen. "Marie Layne," that was my mum's name.

Hilary clicked on the link.

It took them to the death notice for one Marie Layne, nee Cummings. She was buried in Park Lawn Cemetery and predeceased by her husband, Albert, better known as Bert.

The fact they were dead didn't surprise Erik. What surprised him was the sadness he felt because of their loss.

A warm hand touched his thigh. "I'm sorry. You probably didn't want to see that."

Erik took in a ragged breath. She was right. Seeing the deaths of his parents on the computer for all the world to see shocked him. He stood and walked away from the computer and rubbed his eyes with his thumb and forefinger. The news hit him harder than he expected it would. After a few moments of alone time, he returned to Hilary's side. "Can we look for my sister now? It can't be any worse than what we got looking for my parents."

"Sure you're up to it?" she asked, her voice filled with sympathy.

"Might as well get it over with," he said, heaving a sigh.

"And her name?"

"Serenity. Don't know if she's married or not, so best use Layne as her surname."

Hilary typed in Erik's sibling's information. Newspaper headlines popped up on the screen. She clicked on one from *The Globe and Mail,* and a photograph of Serenity accepting an award for *Thacker, Price & Associates* filled the screen.

"All that hard work as a kid paid off, sis. Proud of you," he said.

"She's pretty," murmured Hilary.

"Yeah, she is." As a child, he never thought that way about his sister, but seeing her dressed for the occasion, wearing makeup changed his mind. "Wish I could apologize to her for all the torment I caused her and our parents."

"Maybe you can."

"How? I don't know where she lives."

"This article is from earlier this year. The company Serenity accepted the award on behalf of is a Toronto-based firm."

"And what does that prove?"

"That she's still in the city, or at least was at the time of the presentation."

Erik let Hilary's words sink in. Maybe there was a way of finding and contacting his sister.

"Let's try a lookup of her phone number. We'll start with Canada411.com. If that doesn't work, we'll try something different." Again, Hilary's fingers flew over the keys.

She appeared suited to this type of investigation. Why couldn't she do something similar back on the job? To him, she had a knack for computers and searching. Not all police work happened out on the streets, which is where she wanted to return.

"Sorry. No luck. Your sister's number must be unlisted, or she doesn't have a landline — only a cell."

Erik suffered enough disappointments for one day. Unable to handle any more, he stood, stretched and walked across the room.

"Tell you what. Why don't I ask Luke? I'm sure with the databases the police have access to; he'll be able to find your sister." She picked up her cellphone and punched in his number.

Erik turned around. For a moment, she thought a smile tugged at the corners of his mouth.

"Hi, Luke. It's Hilary. I need a favour. Well, not me, but Erik. He's trying to track down his sister in Toronto."

"Why? So he can make life miserable for everyone?"

Eyebrows knitted into a frown, she looked towards Erik. A combination of anticipation and terror filled his face. She was happy he didn't hear Luke's uncalled for comment.

"Her name is Serenity Layne, and she works, or at least worked, for *Thacker, Price & Associates*. Let me know what you come up with." Before he had a chance to object, she disconnected the call.

"Well?" asked Erik.

"Can't make you any promises, but I think he will. You'll have to be patient, though."

He placed his hands on top of his head. "I suppose. It's been this long already, what's a bit longer."

"That's the spirit. Let's do something to celebrate."

Des met him when he arrived at Onsite. "Where you been?"

"Just came from my methadone treatment."

"What about the rest of the day? You weren't around here."

What was the man getting at? He adhered to the house rules to the best of his knowledge. He was making himself useful in the community. Outside the immediate Gastown neighbourhood, but still, he was performing community service. "Helping Hilary with some stuff."

"You need to start spending a little less time with her and start thinking about what you want to do with your life." Des ushered Erik to the small shared kitchen and invited him to sit. He rested his elbows on the table and his chin on one fist.

"I'd like to work with animals, but not at a shelter, especially a high-kill one. End up adopting every last critter there."

"Boarding kennels? Animal hospital?"

"Something like that."

"We'll see what we can arrange." Des stood and left the room.

The man's questions puzzled Erik. He was in Onsite's transitional unit, but this was the first time his ambitions had been brought up. Everyone knew, or at least he thought they knew, that he worked with Xena and brought her from being a rambunctious puppy to a more sedate one. Hilary needed a dog of that disposition now she was injured. The word crippled almost popped into his head, but he banished that thought before it worked its way in entirely.

Eighteen

Hilary's House, East 7th Avenue, Vancouver

Erik turned up at Hilary's shortly after ten o'clock that morning. Each day, he saw an improvement in her mobility. Too bad, he lived so far away. It was a lengthy walk from Onsite to her place.

On this particular day, the cloudless turquoise blue faded into pale blue closer to the horizon. Usually, he never paid his surroundings much attention. At least not before he met Hilary. She marvelled at the sights and sounds of nature. Her flowerbeds, although overgrown due to her lengthy hospitalization, started to take shape using his labour and her instructions.

"Let's do something. Go somewhere," Erik suggested.

"Sounds good. I've been taking advantage of you. Getting you to help with the gardening, weeding and lawn mowing."

"I don't mind. It's not like you're able to do that much — yet." He added the last word as an afterthought, not wanting her to believe he saw her as completely helpless.

"Go for a walk? Sahalli Park is a few blocks east of here."

She ignored his comment, or at least he hoped she had. "Works for me. How about you, Xena? Wanna go walkies?"

The dog jumped to her feet and wagged her tail so hard, her whole back end swayed.

"I know you're going to object, but we're taking the wheelchair."

Hilary turned to him, opened her mouth and closed it again without speaking.

"I don't want you overdoing things. I'll make you a deal. You can walk to the park, maybe a bit through it, but you're riding home."

She rolled her eyes at him but agreed to his terms.

Erik entered the house, retrieved Xena's leash, and folded the wheelchair. Front door locked behind him, he joined them. Once on the sidewalk with the dog's lead clipped to her collar, they set out down the quiet, treelined street. Beyond the roundabout, they met a woman pushing a small child in a stroller.

He slowed his pace when Hilary's breathing became laboured.

"You okay? I can unfold the chair for you."

She looked him in the eye. "No. I'm fine. Really."

Her stubborn streak wouldn't do her any favours.

He steered Hilary across the street into the park and escorted her to the first bench along the path. Xena circled a couple of times then plopped to the ground. "We're stopping here, and you're not walking back to the house." Whether she paid any heed to the latter part of his statement remained to be seen.

In the distance, the blue-green peaks of the Rockies peeked out from between trees and houses. Erik tipped his head back and let the sun warm his face.

"Vancouver is a beautiful city," she whispered.

"You got that right. Too bad I wasted so much of my life since I got here. I want to thank you for opening my eyes to its beauty. Never been to the park where we walked along the water before. Didn't know the place existed. Can't say the same about VGH or the Police Station, though. Been hospitalized for overdoses and arrested for possession more times than I care to count."

"I hope you're able to stay clean this time. You're good for Xena *and* me."

"Likewise. I now have something to focus on. The methadone keeps the withdrawal at bay."

Hilary pulled a bright pink elastic off her wrist and tied her hair into a ponytail. She had been fortunate since her release from the hospital; the weather was favourable. Warm, sunny days, cool evenings and nights, which made the temperature pleasant for sleeping. She still had physio regularly, but walking with her prosthetic limb became more natural as time went on. Because of its weight, she tired more quickly than in the past. A thought swept into her head, and she giggled.

"What's so funny?" Erik turned on the bench to face her.

"Not sure what made me think of it. Picture this. I'm going through security at the airport. I remove my belt, empty my pockets, take off my shoes — all the things you're supposed to. Well, can you imagine the looks when I take off my leg and put the thing on the conveyer to go through the x-ray machine?" She laughed again.

Erik snorted. "Love your bizarre sense of humour. We might have to go somewhere so you can do just that." The words were out of his mouth quicker than intended. He didn't plan on inviting himself to go on a trip with her, no matter how enjoyable travelling with her could be. If such a journey happened great, but it would be her decision — not him initiating things.

Xena growled and leapt to her feet with hackles raised. Erik tightened his grip on the leash. "Shush," he commanded.

The last thing they needed was for her to run off in pursuit of something and not return.

A male Shepherd stood nose to nose with her. The dogs sniffed one another until the owner pulled him back. The dog's whitened muzzle showed the animal's age. "Enough, Duke," he said, wrapping the leather strap around his hand. "Beautiful dog you've got there. Purebred?"

"Thank you, and yes," said Hilary.

"Still quite young, I suspect."

"Eighteen months."

Erik eyed the man with suspicion. The weather was mild, but not shorts and t-shirt weather, which was what this guy wore. The way he looked at Hilary caused Erik to distrust him more with each passing second.

"Zack Daniels." He extended his hand to her. "Hey, you're that cop who got shot and had to have her leg taken."

Denial was a waste of her time and energy. She was a police officer, so the news of her shooting was regularly brought up on television, radio, and the newspapers. The sooner the story was forgotten, the happier Hilary would be. Unfortunately, that didn't look like it would happen any time soon. "That's me."

"Who did your leg? Vancouver Orthopaedic did mine."

The cloying scent of his cologne caught in the back of her throat. Overpowered by the aroma, she coughed. "Sorry, had a tickle." She lied, but her parents brought her up with the belief if you couldn't say anything positive in a situation, it was best to keep quiet.

Zack, that was his name, wasn't it, shifted. Until that moment, she hadn't noticed the man standing in front of her was an amputee. In his case, the amputation was above his knee. She'd had physiotherapy with other amputees, but they were older, and during conversations discovered, most lost their limbs to diabetes. This guy appeared to be fit. "How did you?"

He cut her off before she could finish. "Motorbike accident on the Coquihalla."

Erik watched the exchange between them. Maybe Hilary should get out and mix with people who suffered similar injuries closer to her age. He couldn't deny he was jealous; her physical loss was one thing she had in common with this Zack guy.

"I bring Duke here a couple of times a week for a game of fetch. Never seen you here."

"Haven't been venturing too far from home. If not for my friend, Erik, I'd still be cooped up indoors."

Zack turned and shook Erik's hand before continuing. "Afraid people will look at you like you're a freak. Been there, done that. It gets easier. You know getting out and being with people. Not so long ago, I wouldn't have been caught dead in a pair of shorts. Tried to keep my peg leg hidden."

Hilary smiled.

"You keep getting her out. The best thing you can do."

"I'll do my best."

"Come on, Duke. Let's go home. See you again." With that, dog and master loped off.

When the two were out of earshot, Erik said, "Did you see that? Poor dog only has three legs. I thought I imagined it, but when they left, he has to hop on one back leg."

"I did. I wonder if the pooch was in the accident, too. I mean guys do take their dogs out on their bikes. Seen when things go wrong, too."

Erik couldn't imagine the horrors Hilary would have seen during her time on the police force. Coming across him in one of his not-so-fine moments being one of them. Over time since that initial encounter, he got off the drugs and so far had stayed off them. He intended to remain drug-free.

His timing was far from perfect, but he touched his palm to her cheek and guided her mouth to his. Her lips were soft, and she didn't pull away from him. When their kiss ended, he searched her eyes for an emotional response to their moment. Unable to glean anything from her, he took his hand away, rubbed his palm on his thigh and stared straight ahead. "I'm sorry. I shouldn't have done that." Erik stood and retreated to the far end of the bench, convinced Hilary hated him for kissing her.

"I'm tired. I want to go home. This walk took more out of me than I expected. Besides, by the time you get back to Gastown, it will be time for you to go for your treatment."

She had a point. It was at least a forty-five-minute walk from here back to the Downtown Community Health Clinic on Powell Street. Or was she about to give him the brush off, and this was her polite way of doing so? Erik sucked in a ragged breath. "You agreed on the way here you would ride home." He unfolded the wheelchair and helped her in.

Neither spoke on the return walk to Hilary's. More negative thoughts circulated through Erik's mind. She might not feel the same way about him as he did about her. Perhaps expressing his feelings verbally rather than with a kiss was the prudent thing to do.

After settling her inside, he couldn't vacate her house soon enough. He headed for the front door, but somehow, she got there before him.

"Thanks for today. It was fun. Will I see you again tomorrow?" She stretched up and kissed him on the cheek.

"If you want."

"I want," she murmured.

Nineteen

Hilary's House, East 7th Avenue, Vancouver

Erik trotted down the steps from Hilary's front door. She asked about tomorrow, so he wasn't getting the brush off after all. Hands shoved in his jeans pockets; he worked his way back through a mix of narrow residential and commercial streets until he reached Main Street. Bike shops, car dealerships and service shops, and more lined the busy thoroughfare.

Along the four-lane street, exhaust fumes from gas and diesel vehicles filled the air. Fast food outlets sprinkled at regular intervals provided respite from the pungent odours. Not that Erik was a huge fan of fast food, but the aromas from these establishments were preferable to the others that permeated his system.

Near the overhead enclosed glass walkway for the Expo line, something shiny on the sidewalk caught his eye. At first, he thought the sun reflected off a speck of quartz in the cement, but no. A toonie glinted in the light. Erik bent down and scooped up the coin. The money had fallen from someone's pocket, but for its monetary value, two dollars, no one would consider making an effort to retrieve the cash, if they even realized they lost it — no one but him.

Did he buy something to eat? A bag of chips might be possible if he were lucky. A bottle of water or a soft drink. Or did he put the two-dollar piece away and not spend it.

When he reached Chinatown, the lamp posts changed from green to red. Bronze dragons decorated some of them. He was closing in on Gastown and Onsite.

The awning of a souvenir shop painted like the Canadian flag advertised T-shirts on sale. An unknown force compelled him to enter. The store was crowded, making it challenging to move around. Customers and items for sale jockeyed for position within the narrow aisles. Erik never considered himself claustrophobic, but this store pushed his resolve to its limit.

Determined to escape the confines of the shop, he headed to the door. There, at the end of the check-out counter, stood three gumball machines. One contained brightly coloured licorice, the other jelly beans. He could buy a handful of either for a quarter. The largest one towered over the two smaller ones and held trinkets in opaque plastic egg-like capsules, and other novelties. The price for these was two dollars — the same amount as the coin he picked up and pocketed earlier. Was this machine the reason for his overwhelming desire to enter?

Erik stood in front of the trio of dispensers pondering his decision. Did he or didn't he? He was so wrapped up in his deliberations; any claustrophobic feelings experienced earlier vanished. He clutched the toonie between his right thumb and forefinger. Onsite provided meals so he wouldn't starve if he fell short of money. Sucking in a deep breath, he placed the coin in the slot and turned the handle.

When he lifted the flap, the 'prize' fell into his hand. He closed his fingers around the plastic container and exited the store. Once outside, he walked to a parking meter out of the way of foot traffic and opened his hand. The case held a plastic ring. A red, heart-shaped 'gem' surrounded by a pattern that resembled sparkling, clear stones. Hilary. He would give it to Hilary.

Erik shoved the haul into his pants pocket. The clock indicated almost five o'clock when he reached the Four

Directions Community Economic and Employment Centre. Thanks to spending the time with Hilary, the day flew by. No time to go back to the transitional unit now. His treatment came first. He needed to hurry to the Downtown Community Health Clinic on Powell Street to get there before the medical centre closed.

Once back at Onsite, Erik walked into the transitional unit's small kitchen, grabbed a bottle of water out of the fridge, and strolled to his room where he flopped on the bed on his back. Fingers laced behind his head, the day's events played through his mind. Until today, he never realized how back-breaking weeding flowerbeds was.

His lack of horticultural knowledge didn't help matters. More than once, he tried to yank one of Hilary's ornamental grasses out of the ground. If not for her quick actions, he would have succeeded. Still, it had been pleasant. They laughed over his mistakes. Although difficult for him to do, he let Hilary fetch and carry refreshments. He drew the line at bags of black earth and mulch, undeterred by her protests. For the most part, Xena loafed around on the grass. A few times, she chased the clods of dirt tossed away with the weeds.

Their walk to Sahalli Park had been pleasant. They only got as far as the first bench and Hilary was exhausted, even though she didn't admit the fact. The only unplanned part of their afternoon was meeting Zack Daniels and his dog, Duke. The man was confident — too confident. Something about him bothered Erik. He didn't trust him. Sure the man was an amputee, but that had nothing to do with his anxiety. So was Hilary, for that matter. It made no difference to him that she was missing a portion of her leg.

The day she was shot shattered her confidence. Initially, the idea of Hilary spending time with Zack because of their similar ages and injuries seemed like an excellent idea to Erik. Now he was unsure. How could he voice his concerns to her without sounding like a jealous oaf? Jealousy could be the reason for his uneasiness.

The timing of his kiss was iffy at best. Maybe better had he kissed Hilary before Zack's appearance rather than after. Her lips were soft and tasted of the lemonade she drank while they performed garden work together. She didn't pull away when his mouth made contact with hers. Positive number one. She asked if he'd be over the next day, not him asking her — positive number two.

Was he reading too much into the other man and his coincidental appearance? Zack said he brought the dog to the park a couple of days a week. Today was the first time Erik and Hilary had been there together. It could have been the truth. There was no way to prove otherwise.

Erik's head spun. The sooner he banished all thoughts of Zack Daniels from his head, the better.

A knock on his door brought an end to his musings. "Come in," he hollered and sat up.

The hinges squeaked. Des stood in the opening. "Remember we talked about you wanting to work with animals, either at a boarding kennel or animal hospital?"

"Yeah." Erik rubbed the back of his head. "Why?"

"Good news. Got you in at Northshore Animal Hospital. Nothing fancy to start. Cleaning cages, feeding animals and that kind of stuff."

"Great! When do I start?"

"Next Monday. A couple of weeks to start. See how you'll fit in with the staff and the animals."

Des handed him a sheet of paper with the directions from the Lonsdale Quay Station to the clinic on Bewicke Avenue. "But ... but I can't afford the SeaBus. If I can't get across the harbour to the north shore, I won't be able to work."

"We'll buy you a reloadable Compass card for one hundred dollars. It will be up to you to maintain the balance so you can commute to and from work."

A job. Erik had a real job, well until he screwed up and lost it anyway. He couldn't wait to tell Hilary his brilliant news.

Hilary curled up on the sofa, with a cup of tea on the end table, TV remote in her hand and Xena at her feet. Well, foot. She removed her prosthetic once she settled herself on the couch. The walk today was harder on her than she had expected. Aiming the remote at the screen, she flipped through the channels. Nothing appealed to her.

Erik was a good friend to her since they met again after her hospitalization. He continued to be now. The kiss on the lips was unexpected. A platonic kiss between friends would have been on the cheek.

Zack was handsome and sure of himself. His stature was that of a person who worked out frequently. Before her injury and subsequent hospital stay, she had taken Xena to Sahalli Park but never saw anyone resembling Zack Daniels or Duke. They didn't blend into the scenery. Quite the opposite — they stood out. He claimed to have taken his dog to the park a few times a week. Maybe he was new to the area. It would make sense given the location of the accident that took his leg.

Was there more to Zack Daniels than met the eye? Hilary eased herself over to the nearby roll-top desk. An online search would or at least should churn up something on the man. The police database would be out of the question. Google was the next best thing. She wiggled the mouse, and the screen came to life. After opening her browser, she typed 'Zack Daniels motorcycle accident on the Coquihalla.' A long list of motor vehicle accidents appeared, but she dismissed many because they didn't involve bikes.

Hilary scrolled through the list until she came across a result that looked promising. She curled her legs up in the chair and clicked on the link. 'Motorcyclist severely injured in collision with a large U-Haul rental truck, going the wrong way.' Her eyes remained glued to the computer screen.

Although the article was grim reading, she read the whole thing. Zack came from a well-to-do family, graduated from University, and until after his accident owned Northshore Animal Hospital. A link within the article took her to an updated story. Most of it recapped what she read in the first one, but went on to say that he was forced to sell his business because he became addicted to Oxycodone. He sold the practice to a senior staff member who still runs it. Zack subsequently spent time in extensive rehabilitation to break his addiction to the drug.

She sure knew how to attract the weirdos. What to do? Since she found Erik unconscious from a heroin overdose in Blood Alley, their relationship changed. What started as a police officer calling for help on finding an OD victim had blossomed. Had she done the right thing when she volunteered to guard his hospital room? Had that action formed some form of strange bond between them?

In the beginning, she wanted to look after him because of Taylor's involvement with drugs, and with any luck, get him off the smack. She hadn't succeeded where her girlfriend was concerned. Memories of Taylor flashed back, and she dashed away her tears.

Erik. Hilary had to turn her thoughts back to him and their kiss. Everything about him was an enigma. He had a few specific health issues associated with being an addict and the lack of proper nutrition in the beginning, but once on methadone treatments and eating properly, those problems disappeared.

Her cell phone rang, startling her. Luke's number filled the display. She took a few deep breaths before sliding her thumb across the screen to accept the call. "Hiya," she said.

"How you doing?"

"Fine. You and your family?"

"We're okay."

Her ex-partner sounded off. She didn't press for details.

"Took some time, but I got that information on Serenity Layne you wanted."

"That's wonderful news." At first, Hilary didn't think he was going to do her the favour. With the delay between the time she asked and now, it appeared to be definite. She couldn't wait to tell Erik the news.

"I'll email you the deets. You still using the same personal account?"

"Yup. They've likely frozen or deleted my police account, so it's the only one I have."

After a short pause, Luke came back on the line. "You should have it in a few. Look gotta go. Talk soon."

In the background, a commotion resounded. Crying and screaming. Luke's daughters were fighting. No wonder he sounded rushed and off-handish. She ended the call and switched to the email function on her phone. Within seconds, the message containing Erik's sister's address and phone number appeared on the screen. Did she call Onsite and try to contact Erik or wait until the next day because he was coming over anyway?

A smile formed on her lips. This was the best possible ending to the day. The turmoil of earlier crumbled, lifting a weight from her shoulders.

The news would thrill Erik. Whether he chose to act on it remained to be seen. He had seemed adamant about wanting to make amends with his sister.

Erik broke out in a cold sweat. A job. He never had a job in his life. His specialties lie in theft and drug use — drug use and theft. What if he blew it? There were plenty of drugs in an animal hospital. Could he resist the temptation?

What did he have to offer Hilary? Not much. He was a recovering addict. What if he succumbed to temptation and started using again? He'd be no use to anyone stoned and back on the streets of Vancouver.

The Gastown neighbourhood was where the down-and-outs congregated. Okay, he lived at Onsite, but it was in the middle of the community. Temptation at every corner. He had to be strong for himself and Hilary.

What about Zack? Should he worry about the man? Yes. The guy shared something with Hilary that Erik never would. How could he compete with that? Initially, he thought Hilary spending time with this other man was a good thing. Better than with the people older than her who lost their limbs from disease, not accident. Now, he wasn't so sure.

Erik loved Hilary. Since she rescued him from certain death, his feelings for her deepened. When he was with her, taking drugs was the furthest thing from his mind. Away from her, he struggled.

Suspicious, too. What if arranging the job was a set up for him to fail?

He leaned on the windowsill. Below on the street, the homeless and the drug addicts congregated. Some slept rough under filthy sleeping bags. Others leaned against buildings while still others sat on the ground, staring off into space. Erik knew that appearance all too well. At one time, he was one of them.

The last word on Navarra was he remained in jail awaiting his court date. Justice moved slowly, but as long as the dealer and his cohorts were behind bars, he and Hilary were safe. So were the heroin addicts until someone else moved into the territory to take over Navarra's dubious clientele.

Would she still want to see him if he did something stupid and went back to the drugs? Not likely. He had to stay steadfast and clean for himself and her.

Erik backed away from the window and drew the curtains.

"Someone's in deep thought," Erik said when he walked into Hilary's front room. She sat in front of her computer with her back to the door.

Hilary jumped and whipped around. "You scared me to death."

"Sorry. Didn't mean to. I knocked but no answer. I can see why now. You're miles away."

"Got involved with something here."

"I can see that. You really should keep your front door locked. Anyone could walk in. After all, I did." Erik walked across the room. "Care to tell me what has you so wrapped up?"

"Luke called yesterday. He found your sister's address and phone number."

"The guy is good for something, after all." Erik snickered.

"I know there's no love lost between the two of you, but you could at least show some gratitude." Hilary rested her arm on the back of the chair.

"Sorry."

"I was looking at the building she lives in on street views. Come have a look."

Erik joined her and sat on the arm of the sofa. "Quite the ritzy neighbourhood. She's got to be rolling in it."

"Your sister wouldn't think you'd changed your ways at all if she heard you talking like that."

"True," he said, the sadness in his voice apparent. Erik sucked in a deep breath.

"Why don't you phone her? You can use my cellphone. At least see if she'll speak to you."

"No, you're okay. I don't think I'm ready."

"Too late — already dialled." Hilary handed him the phone.

After five rings, someone picked up at the other end. "Serenity. It's me. Erik, your brother."

The person who answered the call immediately disconnected.

"She hung up," he said dejectedly.

"Try again," Hilary urged and hit the redial button.

"Please, Serenity. Let me explain. Apologize for being a selfish so-and-so. Leaving you to cope on your own."

The result was the same, but this time the hang-up didn't come as quickly. Was Erik's sister giving some thought to his comments?

"Give her some time. She's not seen or heard from you in years. She might not even be sure you're really you. She'll come around."

Hilary's statement made sense. He left home at fourteen, already addicted to heroin, leaving his sister to deal with his mess and their dysfunctional parents.

"Hey, great news," he said, rubbing his hands together while trying to keep his lips from tugging into a smile. At least not yet.

"What?"

"I've got a job! Can you believe it? Me. Erik Layne, a working man."

"Wonderful," she exclaimed as she leapt out of the chair and hugged him. She pulled back and held both his hands in hers. "Where? When do you start?"

"I told Des working with animals at either a kennel or animal hospital appealed to me. Can't do a shelter. Every time an animal's number came up to be put down, I'd be adopting the poor thing to keep it from happening," he chattered.

Erik's excitement knew no bounds. Hilary had a hard time keeping up with him, let alone understanding his babbling. "You did an excellent job working with Xena. You're my dog whisperer." She hoped a slight change in the conversation would slow him down. "So, where is this place?"

Hilary led him to the sofa, and they sat, hands still clasped together. Erik had come such a long way since she first discovered him in the alley. Moments like this made her job worthwhile. She hoped he could cope with commuting, regular hours and everything that went with gainful employment.

"Oh yeah, the place — Northshore Animal Hospital. I have to take the SeaBus, but Des is arranging a loaded Compass card so I can get back and forth across the harbour. Once I'm working, I'll be the one to keep it topped up. At least that's what he said."

Northshore Animal Hospital had a familiar ring to it. The name popped up in something she'd read online recently. She left her laptop running, so as long as she opened new tabs, the piece she read might still be available. Hilary stood and returned to the computer. She clicked the mouse on the open tab starting at the one closest to her search of Serenity's neighbourhood.

"You're sure they said Northshore Animal Hospital?" she asked.

"Yeah, why?"

"You better come and see this."

In seconds, she felt Erik's hands touching her shoulders and his warm breath on her cheek. Hilary pointed to a location near the top of the screen.

"Blah blah blah blah blah," Erik read aloud. "Zack Daniels! What the ...?" His soft touch and warmth vanished. In the reflection of the screen, he stood clenching his fists.

"There seems to be no getting away from him," she sighed. "In a surreal kind of way, I feel like he's stalking me." Hilary rose and faced Erik. "The man doesn't own the place anymore. He sold it. Keep reading."

Erik leaned closer to the computer screen. His head jerked at one point. Hilary suspected the tidbit about Zack's addiction to Oxycodone was the cause. She reached out to place her hand on his back but pulled back.

Talk about one gigantic mess. Hilary doubted Erik could veto the placement. Even though Zack didn't own the practice anymore, did he still spend time there? Wouldn't that be cozy?

"Do you want me to ask Des if he can find me someplace else to work?"

"You don't have to."

"I don't mind. If you're not comfortable, worst he'll say is no. I still have a few more days before I'm scheduled to start work. He's going to help me get my Social Insurance Number and Health Card, too. I'll ask him then."

"Thank you." Did she have the right to ask Erik to give up a job placement just because of the former owner of the animal hospital? Their relationship was nowhere near that level — yet. Besides, the guy might have never gone anywhere near the place. Having to sell off to either finance his drug habit or keep the business up and running would be a blow to his ego. She laced her fingers together and cracked her knuckles.

Twenty

Hilary's House, West 7th Avenue, Vancouver

Hilary waited on tenterhooks for Erik to arrive. He had worked over the Christmas holidays at the animal hospital, ensuring the dogs, cats and other creatures were fed, warm and safe. It was his turn. She had a surprise for him.

Des sided with her, too. He had fast-tracked the processing of Erik's passport and delivered the official document to Hilary. The animal hospital staff was on board with her plan, also. Now, for the delivery. She hoped her gesture pleased him.

The envelope sat on the desk beside her computer. Now that Erik had a Compass card to commute to and from work, he used the city's metro system when he came to see her. It saved a lot of walking. Still, it took about twenty minutes to walk to her house from the Main Street-Science World station, but better that than the thirty minutes traversing the distance from the Broadway-City Hall stop.

The outside light was on, and now with Erik having a key, he could let himself in when he visited. It was almost six-thirty when he entered the front hall.

By now, Hilary was beside herself, ready to burst at any moment. She couldn't keep the secret much longer. He moved about unhurriedly as he removed his shoes and jacket. If she didn't know better, someone had spilled the beans, and he knew her surprise and now was making her sweat. She was doing that all on her own. Outside assistance was not required.

Finally, he walked into the living room and plopped down on the couch beside her. "Today was brutal. I swear every person who owns a St. Bernard in British Columbia came through. Not one wanted to step on the scale, and the technicians aren't strong enough to lift them. Yours truly was volunteered to do the grunt work."

His complaint about the day left her a way to start the conversation. "How would you like to have a short break? Let your back and other muscles recover."

Erik turned to her and frowned. "What are you talking about?"

"This." Hilary scooped the envelope off the desk and thrust the package towards him.

"What's this?"

"Open it." She squirmed on the sofa as she spoke.

The plain brown envelope held no clue to its contents. She didn't fasten the seal but tucked the flap inside. With the same agonizingly slow speed as before, Erik opened the package then turned it upside down.

Hilary chewed on her bottom lip as the contents dropped into his lap. The first thing to fall out was a passport, followed by a folder emblazoned with the name and logo of a travel agent.

Puzzled, Erik picked up the passport and opened the travel document to the identification page. His credentials stared back at him. The photograph made him appear like a criminal who should be doing hard time as a guest of Her Majesty, not someone about to go off on holiday. At least that was the only reason he could come up with for the remaining contents of the envelope.

"What's this?" he asked.

"Look at it, will you?"

Erik opened the folder and pulled out the paperwork. An airplane ticket. Vancouver to Toronto return.

"I bought it for you so you can see your sister. I have one, too. We're going together."

"But ..."

"No buts."

"I can't afford this."

"My treat."

He swallowed hard, then said, "I can't let you pay for my airfare."

"Look. I got a substantial settlement from the force. I'll never live long enough to spend the entire amount, and isn't the transitional unit at Onsite supposed to be about reconnecting with family? I took care of that for you."

"Still, I don't feel right letting you pay."

"We're friends, aren't we? Then let me do what friends do for each other. I've got your back, the same as you have mine. It started from the moment I found you in Blood Alley."

Erik reached out and took her hand. His eyes burned, and he blinked back tears so she wouldn't see how her gesture affected him. No one had ever done anything like this for him. She was special.

"But ..."

"Now what?"

"Do you really think Serenity will talk to me, let alone see me? We didn't part company on the best of terms. And my job. I can't just up and disappear. What about Onsite? My methadone?"

Hilary shifted on the sofa and leaned closer to Erik. "Are you trying to make excuses, so you don't have to make the trip?"

"N-no."

"Look, I've arranged everything. The staff at the animal hospital are pleased for you. Their way of saying thank you for everything you did over the Christmas break so they could spend time with their families." Hilary stopped talking long enough to take a breath. "We're only gone for a few days. Des arranged for you to receive your treatments at Toronto

General."

"What about Xena? You can't take her on a plane."

"Luke is taking her for the duration. I'll owe him big time when we get back."

She might be excited about the trip, but truth be told the prospect terrified him. How could he tell her he was petrified of being stuck in a cigar tube with wings? He'd never flown except when stoned, but his feet remained on the ground on those occasions.

The following morning, Erik met Hilary at her house, and they took a Black Top taxi from there to the Broadway-City Hall Canada Line station. From here, it was about a twenty-minute commute on the Sky Train to the airport. Two rooms were booked in Toronto at a hotel a few blocks from where Serenity lived. Hilary planned everything to the letter. Nothing could go wrong.

At the airport, Erik passed the walk through the metal detector. Hilary's turn was next. She set off the alarm. A female security officer motioned her to one side. "I have an artificial leg," Hilary said, her voice shaky.

"We have to screen your prosthetic for explosives."

"What do you need me to do?"

"Are you all right to stand or would you like a chair?"

"Prefer to sit if possible."

Another security official brought over a chair for her.

Erik had collected his belongings from the conveyor and started towards her, but the agent motioned him away. Hilary nodded towards him.

"Can you raise your pant leg so I can swab your prosthetic?"

At least she didn't have to take it off. Sure, she joked with Erik about doing just that and seeing the expressions on the faces of the people in the airport — security and passengers both. But she was happy they didn't require such an extreme measure. That would have been embarrassing, not to mention degrading.

The sampling revealed no trace of explosives and Hilary was sent off. In the meantime, Erik gathered her things and re-packed them along with his own.

"Are you up for walking or do you want me to find a wheelchair?" he asked.

"I'm fine. I have to get used to walking longer distances sooner than later."

Luckily, their gate was not far from the security checkpoint.

Hilary sighed and collapsed into a seat in their departure lounge. The walk tired her more than she expected. A lighter-weight prosthetic would have made walking less tiring.

About an hour after they sat, the first boarding call boomed over the speaker — people travelling with small children and others needing assistance.

"Do you want to go now?" Erik asked.

"No. I'll board when they call our section. I don't want any preferential treatment."

Soon they were settled on the plane. Erik next to the window and Hilary along the aisle so she could straighten her leg with ease if required. She relaxed against the arm of the seat between them. He took her hand in his and held it tightly.

They hadn't started to move, and Erik held her in a vice-like grip. She didn't complain. He had never flown before and was nervous, but if his handhold was this tight before they started to move, what was it going to be like when they did? She rested her chin on the palm of her other hand and chewed her bottom lip, hoping he didn't see.

Her worst fear came true when they pushed away from the gate. Erik's grasp tightened.

The jet hurtled down the runway picking up speed for takeoff. Hilary swore she heard her knuckles crack over the roar of the engines. If he soon didn't let go or at least soften his hold on her, the first place they would be visiting in Toronto would be the hospital having her broken hand repaired.

After they reached their cruising altitude, Erik steadily loosened his grip until he let go of her. Hilary moved her hand away from the armrest and flexed her fingers, trying to

eliminate the pins and needles prickling now her blood once
again circulated.

Twenty-One

Pearson International Airport, Toronto

Four and a half hours later, their plane touched down on the tarmac. Erik held her hand in a death grip again. Relief washed over Hilary when they pulled up to the gate and came to a stop. Only then did he relinquish his hold on her.

With only cabin luggage, they didn't have to wait in the baggage hall for their suitcases to make it to the carousel. That saved them about an hour. Still, it took them that length of time to go from the airport to their hotel located a few blocks away from Serenity's condo. Hilary hoped the siblings would reconcile once they had a chance to sit and talk, discover who they now are as opposed to who they were.

When the two reached the check-in desk, Hilary said, "Reservation for Dunbar."

The black-haired clerk wearing too much makeup searched the computer. "One room with two beds for three nights."

"No. The reservation I made was clearly for two rooms with one bed each for three nights." The hairs on Hilary's neck bristled.

"Sorry, but our system isn't showing those details."

"I want to speak to the manager."

So far, the only good thing to come out of the foul-up with the reservation was the fact there were two beds and not just one. Still, Hilary wanted answers.

A tall, slim, bearded man, greying temples and facial hair approached. His skin tone said East Indian. The gold nameplate on his lapel read Narinder Khera, Manager confirming Hilary's thoughts as to his origins.

"What seems to be the problem, miss?"

"The problem is, I reserved two single rooms, and now I have one queen with two beds. My confirmation states that." She whipped her phone out of her pocket and scrolled through the emails until she reached the one she wanted. "See? Two singles."

"I'm sorry, miss. We've had computer problems of late. Perhaps your reservation was caught up in one of the crashes."

"This is unacceptable," Hilary stated, the volume and tone of her voice changing as she spoke.

"It'll be okay, Hil. We'll make it work." Erik turned to the manager. "I'm sorry for the fuss," he apologized.

"It's far from okay, but I don't want to make an even bigger scene here in the lobby."

The check-in process continued, and they took the keycards to their room on the fifteenth floor.

A stack of newspapers sat on the counter. Hilary snatched up a copy of *The Globe and Mail* as she passed.

Despite the glitch with the booking, the room was spacious and airy. A welcome message personalized to Hilary filled the enormous wall-mounted TV screen. As much as she wanted to blame the hotel staff for the error, maybe she was the one to blame. Maybe she clicked on the wrong room when she was on the website. There was nothing she could do about it now, so she resigned herself to making the best of it.

"Window or wall," she asked, staring out the large window.

"Either," said Erik as he dropped their bags on the bed closest to the door. "What have you got in there? Rocks? Your bag weighs a ton."

A wide grin appeared on his face when Hilary turned around. She picked up a small throw pillow and tossed it at him.

Erik whipped it back before lunging towards her and began tickling her. Hilary shrieked and tried to escape, but he held fast and tickled more. The two collapsed on the bed in a fit of giggles.

Their manic moment stopped. Erik rested his right hand on her side and propped himself on his left elbow. He tenderly stroked the hair off her face with that hand. His hazel eyes bored through her, making her heart race, and her breath quicken.

Before she had a chance to react, he mashed his mouth on hers in a deep kiss. At the same time, he pulled her to him and held her there. He tickled her mouth open with his tongue and worked his knee between her legs.

Dizzied by feelings long since dormant, she let herself go and melted into the body next to her. Within seconds, Erik leapt from the bed.

"I-I'm sorry. I got carried away. I shouldn't have taken advantage," he babbled.

Stunned by his sudden reaction, Hilary couldn't speak. She sat and spun around on the bed facing the window. Her mouth moved, but no words tumbled out. Erik stood with his back to her, his hands on his head.

Did he stop because he realized he was about to make love with a defective woman? Or was it because he was a gentleman and didn't capitalize on one of her weaker moments? Neither was good, but at least the latter was palatable.

She climbed off the bed and walked to where he stood. Arms encircling his waist, she laid her cheek against his back. They stood in silence for a few moments, then Erik turned around. The top of Hilary's head rested just below his chin. He wrapped his arms around her and held her close. It was their unspoken apology over the actions following their pillow fight.

"I didn't handle that well," Erik said. "I'd love to make love to you, but the time isn't right, and I mean it isn't right for *you*. I don't want to take advantage, but if I continued, that's what I would be doing. I may do a lot of things, but not that."

Hilary wanted to believe him. So far, he had been truthful with her — at least she thought so. Before the shooting, she was fit and healthy, both mentally and physically. Not anymore.

Fleeting moments of her former self broke through periodically, like downstairs at reception. Still, she was no longer the woman she was when she graduated police college at the top of her class. Not the same steadfast constable she was in her previous life. That was it. Old Hilary — strong, dedicated, and full of life. New Hilary — weak and paralyzed by fear and self-loathing.

"Should soon think about heading off for my methadone treatment." Erik adjusted his position and pulled Hilary closer to him. "Trouble is, I don't want to let go of you."

"Nor me, you." She nuzzled into the hollow of his neck.

Erik wound his grey scarf around his neck and shrugged into his black leather jacket. Hilary followed suit. Her bright orange pashmina accented her complexion and dark eyes. The cane he insisted she brought with her stood propped against the end of the television stand. Erik nodded towards it. He grabbed it when she ignored him. "You're taking it with you," he insisted. "I know Toronto. Trust me. You'll be glad you have it."

She responded with a roll of her eyes but took the walking stick from him.

When the elevator doors opened, they left the hotel and started down Bay Street. Much like Vancouver, high rises lined the streets. Some were a combination of retail and residential. Others housed multi-storey office buildings. Beyond Bloor Street, a substantial Indigo Bookstore took up a good chunk of the expanse on their left.

They continued down the street. The lengths of the blocks varied. Some were quite long; others short. In the distance, a car backfired. Hilary stiffened then began to shake violently. Erik led her to a bench by a green space where she could sit. He joined her and enveloped her in his arms. She peered around him, trying to determine if she was safe and if the gunman was after her. Her fingers dug into Erik's arm. Her psychologist told her to expect occurrences such as this. Tears streamed down her face, and she was powerless to stop them.

People walking by on the sidewalk stared at her. Their gazes made Hilary uncomfortable. It was like she was on display. The one-legged freak cop from Vancouver. A circus sideshow act.

Gradually, Erik's embrace calmed her. Ragged breaths from her bout of tears made her chest ache.

"We're not going anywhere until you're ready," he said.

"B-but, your t-treatment," she gasped.

He rubbed Hilary's back as he spoke. "When I'm with you, I'm fine. I don't need the methadone."

The cop in her emerged. Too many addicts who missed their treatments wound up back on heroin. She had witnessed it many times during her time on the Vancouver Police force.

Erik helped Hilary stand and wrapped a protective arm around her shoulders. "You're safe with me. I won't let anything happen to you." He squeezed her gently, pulling her closer to him. Her free arm encircled his waist.

Had he fallen in love with her — his rescuer? If she didn't find him unconscious in Blood Alley, he wouldn't be here today, walking down Bay Street in Toronto with her in his arms. Strangely, it was Nightingale Syndrome, except for her profession. She never once rebuffed him, although he presented her with many opportunities. Did she feel the same way about him as he did her? They shared a passionate moment before he decided the timing was wrong.

When they reached the hospital, it took some time to find the department where Des had arranged for Erik to get his treatments while away from Vancouver.

Hilary leafed through an issue of *Toronto Life* while they waited, glad of the chance to sit and rest. She barely looked up when a nurse called Erik's name. Even though the magazine was a few months old, the articles held Hilary's interest. One, in particular, drew her in more so than the others. She was so engrossed in it; she didn't hear Erik return.

"Ready to go?" he asked.

She leaned down and shoved the magazine in her oversized crossbody bag. "Reading material for later. I want to finish the piece I started."

A grin formed on Erik's face. "You a cop and you're a klepto."

"Shh. Don't want my secret getting out."

Erik helped her into her coat, and they left. Once outside, the two broke into laughter — deep belly laughs to the point Hilary snorted.

About halfway between the hospital and the hotel, they stopped at a pizzeria for a bite to eat. They ordered the pizza and wings combo with soft drinks and dipping sauces.

"Anyway, I wanted to keep the magazine because there's an article on house prices and what's available in that range. I thought the housing market in Vancouver had gone crazy." Hilary stopped talking long enough to take a sip of her pop. "Toronto is just as bad. Around a million for small houses with no land. And if you want bigger and a bit of grass to cut, a back lawn for kids to play in, you're talking multi-millions. The world has gone nuts."

Erik wiped his mouth with his napkin. "I can't imagine the house we lived in on Islington being worth those kinds of dollars. Wouldn't be surprised if it was torn down. It wasn't in the greatest shape back then. Everyone in the neighbourhood struggled when the plant closed."

A nostalgic look appeared on his face. Hilary never experienced a childhood like his, so any sympathy expressed was hollow. At least she figured he would see it that way.

"Stoner, is that you?" a man wearing jeans and a grubby T-shirt asked. His arms, covered with sleeve tattoos, added to his general unkempt appearance: dirty fingernails, greasy hair and scruffy moustache.

The voice was familiar, but it took some time before Erik was able to put the face and name to it. "Rocky?"

"Yup."

Erik stood and embraced the man. "Been a long time."

"Too long. Where did you disappear to?"

"Vancouver."

"Wanna go out and catch up on old times? Maybe shoot a little tar?"

Hilary's expression said, 'if you do, you're on your own.' Of course, he would be. She took a chance on him, and he couldn't revert to his old ways. Not now, even though he was back in the Big Smoke.

"Who's the broad? She's quite the looker," the scruffy man said.

"Her name is Hilary. She helped me get my life back on track."

"Wouldn't mind a piece of the action, if you know what I mean."

"Back off, Rock. She's a cop."

"No way."

Hilary stood. "Yes, way."

The unkempt man backed a few steps away from them. "You're sleeping with a pig?"

Erik stepped forward until he was nose to nose with the man. "It's none of your business if I am or not, but you'll *not* refer to her that way. Understand?" He leaned forward, making the other man shrink away.

"I-I, sorry. Didn't mean to cause any harm. Guess that means we're not going to shoot up any smack." He turned and scuttled out of the eatery.

"Sorry about that. I should have known being here meant there was a good chance we'd run into one of my old drug buddies."

"You didn't take off with him. That's a wonderful sign." Hilary smiled.

Her dark eyes sparkled, and dimples formed in her cheeks. She was gorgeous, and she was with him. As long as they were together, Erik swore he would stay off the drugs. His days of existing in a drug-induced stupor on the streets of Gastown were over. "Let's go back to the hotel. I've had enough of Toronto for today."

Hilary nodded and picked up her cane.

Back at the hotel, Hilary flipped through the copy of *The Globe and Mail* she picked up earlier at reception. She perused the real estate section, and an address caught her attention. It couldn't be. Could it? She reached for her smartphone and scrolled through her emails until she found the one from Luke with Serenity's address. Her eyes darted back and forth from newspaper to phone, taking in the information. The two addresses matched. "Erik," she hollered.

He came into the room, bath sheet wrapped around his waist, drying his head with another towel. "What's up?"

"Only the perfect way to set up a meeting with your sister."

"Huh?"

Hilary scrambled off the bed with the newspaper page in one hand and her phone in the other. "Look, here. There will be an open house at Serenity's condo on Monday. It works out great. We don't fly back to Vancouver until the day after that."

"What are you on about?"

Frustrated with his lack of comprehension, she poked him with her phone. "We go to the open house."

"Yeah, I get that. But isn't it customary for the homeowner to be away from the property during such an event?"

"So, we stay behind. There will be enough interest that the

real estate agent won't be able to keep track of everyone. We'll hang back, and when he or she locks up after the perceived last prospective buyers have left, it's a waiting game until Serenity comes back."

"But what if she doesn't? What if she's off on a business trip or something?"

"According to what we found online about your sister and the additional information I got from Luke, Serenity is just back from spending six months on the road. She's not going to want to be going anywhere. Not when she has this posh condo. I know if it was me and I had been away for so long, spending quality time in my place with my things would be at the top of my list. Become a hermit of sorts."

Erik couldn't argue with Hilary's logic. If he phoned his sister, she'd hang up immediately like she did when he tried from Vancouver. What if Serenity called the police and had them charged upon discovering them in her home? Still, he needed to make amends — or at least try. That was part of the Onsite mandate. Help residents find employment and reconnect with families.

What about the legal aspect of what Hilary suggested? Once the tour ended, they had to leave like everyone else, not stay behind. They weren't exactly breaking and entering, but trespassing. If Hilary were to get arrested, any chance of her returning to her job with the Vancouver Police Department vanished.

"I'm not sure I like this idea. What if Serenity calls the police? What if we get arrested? You'll never return to work."

"Fussbudget. You worry too much." Hilary picked up a small pillow and tossed it at him. "My turn in the shower now."

Hilary gathered her toiletries and a pair of flannel pyjamas and headed into the bathroom. While she waited for the water to get to the right temperature, she removed her prosthetic limb and sock and propped it in the corner with the latter stuffed inside the cup.

The shower had grab bars, but she still had to sit on the side of the tub, then swing around and clutch the safety devices before she was able to stand. It was awkward but achievable. Her routine here wasn't so different from that at home. There, she had a standalone shower in addition to a bathtub in her townhouse.

"Your sister certainly made a name for herself," Hilary whispered. She and Erik lingered at the end of the line of prospective buyers.

"That she has."

Sleek living room furnishings made for clean lines. The decor was tasteful yet minimal. Hilary's decorating tastes were different from Serenity's. Hilary filled her home with overstuffed, chunky, sofas and chairs. The kind you sank into and didn't want to leave, bright colours, not to mention dog toys and other canine accessories. Throw in a tumble dog or two that mysteriously appeared from time to time, and the style was complete. Hilary referred to the dust bunnies in that fashion because they were courtesy of Xena. Still, she couldn't imagine life without her beloved pet.

The tour progressed through the condo to the kitchen. White cabinets, black granite countertops, and stainless-steel appliances hugged the walls. In the middle of the room stood a small island. Pot lights dotted the ceiling and an industrial-looking fixture with three lamps hung in the centre of the room.

From what Erik said about the family, his sister didn't have much use for him, right from the time they were small children. It might come down to her negotiating abilities to keep them from being turned over to the authorities should things go pear-shaped.

Casually, people filed out of the bedroom. It was big, but only so many people could fit in there at one time. Two couples waited ahead of them to tour the room.

When they finally got through the doorway, Erik nudged Hilary to the far end of the room. A huge tallboy provided cover. She pressed herself against the wall and pulled him back, too. The piece of furniture had to be six feet tall and over two feet deep. A dresser with a mirror affixed to it stood on the other side of the room next to a tub chair under the window, the latter occupied by a bedraggled stuffed animal. At least they were out of range of the looking glass.

It seemed like hours before the front door closed, and she and Erik were the only ones in the condo. Hilary exhaled the breath she held since hiding behind the chest of drawers.

Maybe all the things Luke said about Erik were right? He would never amount to anything. He'd drag her down to the gutter with him. It was starting that way.

But, he was good with animals. With the help of Des and the Onsite program, he had a meaningful job at Northshore Animal Hospital. Xena loved him. She gave him a purpose, and since his time in rehab both as an inpatient and out, he changed. Deep down, she knew he had turned the corner and was ready to embrace a life without heroin, and she was pretty sure, she and her dog would be part of that life.

A key scraped in the lock. A doorknob turned. Footsteps and something on wheels rolling across the floor. The clatter of metal dropping into a bowl. Hilary gasped. Serenity was home.

Twenty-Two

Serenity's condo, Yorkville Avenue, Toronto

Serenity turned the key in the deadbolt. A sliver of light glowed beneath the door. The realtor must have forgotten to turn off one of the fixtures. Or, she was still showing the property and extolling the virtues of residing in this trendy borough.

She pulled her rolling computer bag through the foyer behind her into the empty room. No one was in the kitchen, either. Still, someone was inside. She was sure of it. Boots removed and slippers on, Serenity moved cautiously around the living room.

Before going any further, she grabbed an overweight sculpture off the coffee table. If someone were in her home, they'd regret it.

On tiptoes, she crept down the corridor towards the bathroom. The clear glass shower doors prevented anyone from hiding there. A shuffling sound came from her bedroom. She took a deep breath and flung open the door.

Space customarily occupied by her tatty panda bear sat conspicuously empty. A man stood in front of the dresser with his back to her.

"Don't move. I called the police." The threat was empty. She didn't dial 9-1-1, but the intruder didn't know any different.

He turned around and faced her.

"My God, Erik. What are you doing here?"

"Nice to see you, too, sis."

"What? How?" she babbled.

"Before I tell you that, there's someone I want you to meet." He motioned to the corner.

A woman with jet black hair appeared from around the dresser. She walked with an awkward gait, and the cane she carried didn't seem to be of much help. Slowly, she worked her way to Erik's side, and he wrapped his arm around her waist.

"This is Hilary," he said, "and this is my sister, Serenity."

Now the social niceties were aside; the time came to find out what on earth was happening.

"Can we go through to your living room and sit down?"

Pain etched the woman's ebony eyes. Serenity extended her arm, inviting them to leave the sanctity of her bedroom. As Erik walked past, she yanked her stuffed animal away from him.

Once in the living room, Serenity waited for her two uninvited houseguests to sit before taking a seat in the armchair facing them. "Do you mind telling me exactly what you are doing in my home?" Her biting tone meant business.

Hilary massaged her thigh. Was it a nervous reaction?

"I'm waiting."

"Been in Vancouver for about twenty years," said Erik.

"No doubt, stoned out of your mind on something." Serenity tightened her grip on the panda bear in her lap.

"Yeah." Erik hung his head; his voice sheepish. "But Hilary found me and saved me."

"What do you mean, found you and saved you?"

"I got into some bad heroin. If Hilary didn't spot me unconscious in Blood Alley, I'd be dead."

The hairs on the back of Serenity's neck bristled. "And

just what was she doing there?"

"I am in the room. If you must know, my partner and I were out on routine patrol ..."

"What's this nonsense?"

"I am a constable with the Vancouver Police Department ... well until I was shot in the line of duty."

"Back up. I'm confused."

Erik squirmed on the sofa then stood. "I was in a bad place back then. Spent a long time in hospital and rehab, but I'm clean now and have been for going on eight months. Well, I'm on methadone, but that keeps the withdrawal symptoms away, so I don't miss the smack. I even have a job. Been working at Northshore Animal Hospital pretty much since I went to the Onsite facility — a rehab/re-entry house. Hilary has supported me and thanks to her, the dealer who provided the tainted smack is now behind bars."

"He is clean. That's the truth. He's been a great support to me, too, since the shooting. We ended up on the same floor in Vancouver General — Mental Health and Substance Use. I needed counselling after I lost my leg. No beds were available in the surgical ward, so they stuffed me in that unit. Erik was still undergoing his treatment as an inpatient, and our paths crossed again."

The story sounded so far-fetched; it had to be true. It couldn't be made up. The two sitting in front of Serenity proved the adage, truth is stranger than fiction. "So, you said you were a cop until the shooting. What happened?"

"Sis," Erik protested.

"Don't worry. I would rather have things out in the open anyway." Hilary raised her pant leg and removed her prosthetic lower leg, her left extremity missing from just below the knee. She sighed and adjusted the sock over her stump. "You asked. Here's what happened. The bullet entered my lower leg, and caused so much damage; the injury was non-repairable. It was either the leg or my life."

"What can I say?" Serenity's cheeks grew hot with embarrassment.

"Your brother has been a star. He's helping me regain my

independence, working with my dog, Xena, and training her as a service dog. She failed miserably at becoming a police dog."

"You two are in a relationship?"

"We're friends. Good friends."

The way the two looked at one another made Serenity suspect there was more to their situation than friendship. An invisible bond existed between her brother, this woman and her dog. The only thing missing was a child. Otherwise, it was her and Roger all over. "I'm sorry. I think you better leave. Leopards don't change their spots, Erik Layne, and I don't believe you have either. Too much happened before you left home for me to forgive you. You'll be back on the drugs and stealing from people to support your habit again in no time."

"But …"

"No." Still clutching her stuffed animal, Serenity swept across the room to the door. She yanked it open and stood aside so they could leave.

Erik stood and helped Hilary with her prosthetic. When they reached the door, he shot his sister a pleading look.

"Thanks for not getting the police involved," said Hilary, following Erik out the door. "It was lovely to meet you. And if it means anything, I trust your brother. I'll help him stay clean."

"Just go. Now."

Serenity pushed the door shut as soon as her visitors exited her condo. She leaned back and stared at the ceiling. Of all the times for her brother to turn up. A strip needed to be torn off the realtor for letting it happen. The woman should have been more responsible and checked all the rooms to ensure everyone had vacated before leaving to go to her next showing. Was throwing her brother and his lady friend out of her home the right thing to do?

Dejected by the outcome of his visit with his sister, Erik schlepped around the hotel room, gathering his belongings. One by one, he stuffed them into his duffel bag. He was sad and angry at the same time and had desperately wanted to show

Serenity he had changed — and for the better.

"Hurry up. We have to be at the airport at least two hours before our flight."

"I can't help thinking this whole thing's been a mistake. A mistake that cost you a bundle of money."

Hilary wrapped her arms around his waist and rested her cheek on his back. "At least now, you know. I told you before I'm not worried about you paying me back. It's my way of thanking you for being next to me through the rough patches and sticking with me."

Erik turned and tipped her chin up with his thumb and forefinger. "I appreciate your efforts. Believe me." He bent down and kissed her forehead.

Bag zipped shut, he held the door for Hilary, and they made their way downstairs and checked out of the hotel.

A short walk to the Bloor-Yonge subway station under gloomy, gunmetal grey clouds didn't improve Erik's mood. If it wasn't for Hilary being with him, he might have kicked or punched something or someone to vent his frustrations.

The underground stop was directly in front of the train terminal. Union Station filled the block on the south side of Front Street. The immense structure never ceased to take Erik's breath away — even on a dreary day. On the outside, the stone building looked more like a palace than a transportation hub. Inside, the concourse was every bit as impressive. Round-topped windows at either end of the great hall, along with other windows in the front façade, filled the room with natural light. The marble floor shone like a fresh coat of ice on a pond.

They walked across the concourse to the platform where the UP Express train would shuttle them to the airport. With nothing to tie him to Toronto anymore, Erik couldn't wait to board the plane and return to Vancouver. On the west coast, he had a job, a roof over his head, and the woman now beside him who might want to become more than just a friend.

Terminal three at Pearson was its usual hectic place. It took forever to find their check-in desk, and then the line queued back and forth between the barriers. Had the airline overbooked the flight? They had legitimate tickets for their return to Vancouver.

When they eventually checked in, Hilary heaved a sigh of relief. They weren't bumped due to overbooking. The airline employee handed them tags for their cabin luggage. Once they had those in hand, they worked their way through the crowd of passengers, people saying farewell, and the sea of unfamiliar faces.

Hilary held both boarding passes in the inside pocket of her leather jacket. If something separated them before security, Erik would have to wait for her to catch up. He didn't fly well on the flight to Toronto, and that was with her by his side. She followed the back of Erik's head, cutting through the crowd. Thankfully, he had both bags — one slung over his shoulder and the other in his hand. At least he started with two pieces of baggage.

Difficult as it was to keep up, Hilary did her best. Jostled and bumped by people moving faster than her, she cursed her disability. At times, the temptation to clobber someone with her cane rose to the surface.

She approached the entrance to the security hall. Erik stood to one side. "Sorry about that. A herd of inconsiderate clods got between us. I had to keep moving at their pace or be trampled," he said, putting his arm around her shoulders.

"You're not telling me anything I don't know. What is it about airports that makes people so rude?"

"Shall we?"

"Yes. The sooner I can sit down and rest, the better."

Erik released his grip and took Hilary's hand as they walked towards the stanchions separated by dark blue straps. Inside the back and forth maze designed for crowd control, the pair took a couple of steps. Stopped and waited, then moved again.

Someone official near the doors hollered instructions. "Computers, tablets and cellphones out of your bags."

Hilary pulled her computer out, closed her bag and shuffled it forward with her feet.

A woman's voice wafted over the din of people grumbling and luggage being zipped and unzipped. Briefcase latches clicking open added to the cacophony. "Erik. Erik Layne. Wait!"

"Did you hear something?" asked Hilary.

"Yeah, but not sure what."

Again someone called his name.

He spun around and scanned the space for the source of the sound. There, coming on the run, was Serenity waving her arms. "Erik, please wait. I've been a fool."

Erik ducked under the retractable straps and raced towards his sister. The eyes of everyone else in the building stared at them. Did they think he and his sibling were a couple? When they met, he bear-hugged her, lifting her off the ground.

Hilary soon caught up with him. Breathless, she panted, "Sorry. I couldn't cut through like you. Had to come around the long way." Her comments fell on deaf ears. Erik and Serenity were so engrossed in one another.

"Erik, I'm so sorry about the other day. I was wrong. I spoke with Roger, and he convinced me not to leave things as they were when I sent you packing." A tear slid down her cheek, and he brushed it away.

"Roger? Who's this Roger character?"

"He's a friend, a good friend, who lives in Québec City. I met him when I worked my last assignment for *Thacker, Price & Associates.* I'm moving there at the end of the month, which is why I'm selling my condo."

"Wow. I never figured you for the soppy type, sis." Erik stepped back and held his sibling's hands. The woman in front of him under his scrutiny was his sister. A robotic Stepford Wife hadn't replaced her, nor was she taken over by Body Snatchers.

A garbled announcement came over the speakers.

"That's us," Hilary said. "They're paging us to go to the gate. We've got to go."

Erik turned to her then back to his sister. The wall she built to protect herself had started to crumble. She'd let a man into her life. "We've got to …"

Serenity pulled a business card and ballpoint pen out of her handbag. "My email and phone number so we can keep in touch," she said, scribbling on the piece of card stock. "Please, call or email me. I want to keep in touch with you — both of you."

One last hug and Erik and Hilary raced to security. More, he ran and tugged her along behind him.

As soon as they passed security, the driver of one of the golf cart-like vehicles picked them up and whisked them to their gate.

Twenty-Three

Onsite Detox Transitional Unit, East Hastings, Gastown, Vancouver

The new year started with a bang. The trip to Toronto with Hilary. His reconciliation with his sister. A pay raise from the animal hospital. At this rate, he would soon be able to move out of the re-entry house and get a place of his own. Something small. A bachelor apartment would do.

Until this year, he never gave real estate prices or the cost of renting a second thought. Hilary got him thinking about it: thanks to the magazine she liberated from the clinic at Toronto General Hospital, where he went for his methadone treatments.

There was only one thing that would make life better at this point — spending more time with Hilary.

Erik rummaged in the nightstand. Not there. Next, he rooted in the top drawer of the highboy. Tucked away in the back corner, he found the plastic container. The gumball machine ring he bought the day he found the toonie on the ground on his way back from Hilary's.

His schedule was such at Northshore Animal Hospital; he worked a lot of Saturdays and Sundays. Days off usually fell mid-week. Tuesday-Wednesday or Wednesday-Thursday. He consulted the calendar he kept track of his hours on. He was off on the fifteenth. He'd do it then. He hoped he could wait that long.

The days crawled by. Finally, January 15th arrived. He went for his methadone treatment first thing in the morning. After, he walked to Waterfront Station, where he caught the Expo line to the stop at Main Street and Terminal Avenue. From there, it was a twenty-minute walk to Hilary's. All he had to do was persuade her to accompany him to Gastown.

Luck was on his side, and Hilary was game to get out of the house for some of winter's fresh air. Any other time and they could have brought Xena with them, but travelling on the metro made it impossible. On second thought, Erik had never seen a dog on the trains or in the stations. Not even service dogs. It could have been nothing more than timing that prevented his seeing people with their canine companions.

"You warm enough?" he asked her shortly after they left her house.

Hilary's cheeks were red from the near-zero temperature. Puffs of steam formed in front of her face every time she exhaled. Erik's breath was visible, too, but he was more concerned for her.

"Yeah, I'm fine."

Thirty minutes after leaving Hilary's, they walked into the metro station. With her not moving as fast as him, it took longer to get to their destination. Under normal circumstances, he traversed the distance in less time than that.

When their train arrived, there was only one seat available. Erik ensured Hilary was comfortably ensconced and stood in front of her, mentally going over his speech. In less than ten minutes, the train slowed for the platform at Waterfront Station. It would probably take longer to get out of the terminal than to their final destination.

People lined outside the train's doors waiting to board, making it difficult for those wanting off to de-train. The same situation held true at the turnstiles, although here, everyone was going in the same direction. The hold-up was not having Compass cards at the ready, or the e-passes were not scanning.

Out on West Cordova Street, Erik heaved a sigh. He took Hilary's hand, and they started down the street past the Steamworks Brew Pub and around the bend on Water Street. His speech was well-rehearsed, but the thought of mucking it up terrified him. Moisture dampened his scarf at the back of his neck as sweat beaded there.

The steam clock finished its proclamation of forty-five minutes past the hour as they approached. The timing was perfect. Erik positioned Hilary next to the timepiece then got down on one knee. "It's not where we first met, but ..."

"What are you doing?"

Erik repeated the first part of his sentence. "... Blood Alley isn't the most romantic location, and we're only around the corner." He cleared his throat and removed her left glove. The plastic capsule containing the piece of jewellery extracted from his pocket, he popped open the outer packaging and placed the ring on her left pinky finger. "I know it isn't real, but one day you'll have a real one. Hilary, will you marry me?"

Hilary clapped her gloved right hand over her mouth. A marriage proposal on Water Street in Gastown next to the steam clock was the last thing she expected. Her cheeks flushed, not from the cold but embarrassment. By now, a crowd of people gathered in a semi-circle around them. "Answer the man," someone said.

"I-I don't know what to say."

"Say yes," urged a young girl in the front row.

The girl bounced up and down, keeping her feet firmly on the ground, whether it was for warmth or excitement from the marriage proposal playing out on the street remained unknown.

Erik, steadfast in front of her on one knee, held her left hand in both of his.

"Are you going to say yes or what? Some of us have jobs. Get on with it," a man near the curb, newspaper tucked under his arm, said.

She leaned down and whispered, "You can get up now."

Once Erik was upright, she threw her arms around his neck. "Yes, of course, I'll marry you!"

He encircled her waist with his arms, lifted her off the ground and spun her around. "She said yes. Did you hear that? She said, yes!"

A round of applause greeted them, which was soon drowned out by the steam clock proclaiming the top of the hour. Its timing was such that it was as if it were pleased, too.

"I love you, Hilary Dunbar. You've made me the happiest man ever," he said when he put her back on her feet.

"And I love you, too, Erik Layne."

He pulled her close, and their lips touched. While in their embrace, a light snow began to fall, making the scene more perfect than it already was.

Epilogue

Hilary's House, East 7th Avenue, Vancouver

September 16, 2018 ...

D-Day. The day of the annual Terry Fox Run. Since the overwhelming urge compelled her to visit the memorial to the teenager, Hilary made up her mind she would take part in this year's run and raise money for the cause.

Her training for the event started in cherry blossom season — the same time she returned to work. She jogged early every morning from her house to Sahalli Park and back. The subtle fragrance of the pale pink flowers energized her.

As she became more fit, Hilary stretched out the run to that park and rather than stop at her house on the return trip; she went on to and around Guelph Park before returning home. Still, she had not grown confident enough to wear clothing which exposed her prosthetic limb, until today.

Hilary stepped into her pale blue shorts and tugged a black, racerback tank top over her head. A hoodie hung on her bed's footboard. She rummaged through her dresser until she found a pair of white sweat pants. If the weather turned chilly, she didn't want to be cold, and if the temperature got too warm, she could take the long pants off, and stuff them in her small backpack.

Arrangements were in place for Erik to meet her and Xena at the registration table. Once Hilary finished signing in for the event, he'd take the dog and go to the finish line and await her arrival.

It was a toss-up which she worked at harder — training for the event, or raising money through sponsorship.

Hilary pulled on the long pants. Her track shoes were well-worn, but today was not the time to start with a new pair. That would be looking for trouble. Another search through the rucksack turned up a small box of name brand sticking plasters in assorted sizes. Running the distance, she planned on; blisters would likely form. The last thing she wanted was to have one break. If that happened, and she had something to prevent further chafing, it wouldn't be so bad.

Registration for the event began at eight o'clock. The glowing numerals on her alarm clock displayed seven-fifteen. On a good day, the drive from her house to Stanley Park, where the race took place, took about twenty minutes.

Dressed in her running gear and her hair tied in a ponytail, she gathered the rest of her things and went downstairs.

Xena lifted her head when Hilary rounded the bottom of the staircase.

"Ready to go, girl? Big day for me."

Wallet and pledge forms shoved in her backpack, Hilary grabbed her keys and Xena's leash. The dog leapt to her feet and wagged her tail furiously. Lead clipped to Xena's collar, the two hurried out the front door.

Aiming her key fob at the car, Hilary unlocked the vehicle and bundled the German Shepherd in from the passenger side. She rounded the Kia Forte, appreciating the fact the car came equipped with an automatic transmission, so even though she lost her left leg, she could still drive. She was grateful, too, that the government didn't revoke her driver's licence because of her amputation.

By the time she arrived at Stanley Park, the dashboard clock displayed almost seven forty-five. Volunteers wearing hi-vis vests directed her to the parking area. From there, it was less than a five-minute walk to the registration desk.

Erik waited there for her as promised. "Hi gorgeous," he said and kissed her on the forehead.

Hilary smiled and handed Xena's leash to him.

People mingled in the section of the park where the race would take place. A number of women dressed in running gear with small children in strollers visited among themselves. The word 'cancer' emanated from the group of young mothers. Hilary turned, but had no way of knowing who, if anyone, suffered from the odious disease. They could have been talking about Terry Fox for all she knew.

During the sign-in process, she turned in her pledge sheets along with the money already collected. There had been no problems getting most of the department to sponsor her, although some cajoling, coercing, and haranguing took place to persuade others to cough up their money. Still, when they made their donations, they were all smiles. Likely, just a wind-up to make her think they wouldn't.

"Which run are you doing?" the young girl at the desk asked.

"The 10K."

Erik asked, "Are you sure? That's quite the distance."

"Yes, I'm sure. You look after Xena and leave the running to me. I've been training for this run since the spring. I'll be fine." What if she wasn't? Had she taken on too much? The other runners appeared to be able-bodied and in possession of their lower limbs, unlike her.

It was just like Erik to worry about her, but at times his over-protectiveness was too much. The run didn't start until ten o'clock, which allowed Hilary plenty of time to warm up. Stretching, running in place — things that would reduce the chance of leg cramps once she started.

Hilary sat her backpack on the ground, unzipped the tiny front compartment and took a handful of bandages out of the box and shoved them in the pocket of her hoodie. She was removing her sweat pants when a familiar voice said, "Hey, glad to see you out. Really out."

She turned. Zack Daniels stood in front of her. His gaze lowered towards Hilary's prosthetic. Erik's arm encircled her waist, and he drew her close to him. Even though she accepted his marriage proposal, there was something about the man facing them that, in Hilary's eyes, made Erik insecure. To ease his worry, she cuddled closer.

The starter summoned the runners to the starting line. "Good luck," Erik said before kissing Hilary on the cheek. "And to you." He extended his hand in a goodwill gesture to Zack.

The men shook hands. "Don't worry; I'll look after her."

His offer to take care of her made Hilary cringe. Erik's face reddened, which said he felt the same.

Erik, shoulders slumped, and Xena walked off.

"Don't start too fast. You'll burn yourself out, and lactic acid will set into your muscles," Zack instructed.

"Oh, shut up. I do know about running." The sooner Hilary escaped from this arrogant guy, the happier she would be. She stretched some more, trying to ignore him.

The race started, and Hilary sprinted ahead. Too fast, but she wanted to get as far away from Zack Daniels as possible. He rubbed her the wrong way, and he had a profound effect on Erik — and not a positive one.

Footfalls sounded from a group of runners behind her and Hilary adjusted her speed to blend in with them. Once in the pack, it would be next to impossible to have unwanted attention lavished on her. Thankfully, Zack wasn't in this group. As long as she could keep pace, this was where she'd stay.

An uneven patch on the path proved to be Hilary's undoing. She caught her left foot and stumbled to the ground. Hands out to break her fall, the palms of her hands and knees scraped on the gravel. Struggling to her feet, she cursed herself for being so clumsy. Blood dripped down her right leg from a cut. Palms scuffed, but her hands didn't bleed. She rubbed them together and carried on. Someone offered her a pre-moistened first-aid wipe.

Without turning to see the wipe's provider, Hilary accepted the small packet.

"Take a minute and clean yourself up. You don't want to get an infection."

That voice. Zack. He'd caught up to her. Blast! What made the situation more irritating was he was right. Hilary moved off to the side of the running area and cleaned her knee. The alcohol in the wipe stung her raw skin, forcing her to breathe through clenched teeth. The beginnings of a bruise formed. She winced when covering the wound with one of the bandages she stashed in her pocket earlier.

Her knees stung and throbbed, especially the right one. No matter how much she wanted to shake off this man, her body was in no fit state to comply — at least not yet. The next best thing was to ignore him, and Hilary could do that quite easily. She got to her feet and eased back into a jog. So far, so good.

A sign ahead indicated the three-kilometre point and the finish line for those only wishing to participate in that length of a run — only seven more to go.

A lawn tractor droned in the distance sending the sweet scent of freshly cut grass into the air. Beds of fragrant autumn flowers added a spicy aroma to the mix.

Zack adjusted his speed to run with Hilary. The man was so sure of himself. Maybe in time, she would regain her confidence. Some of it must have returned because she wore shorts today for the first time in public.

At the five-kilometre mark, more runners dropped out. Unfortunately, for Hilary, her running partner wasn't one of them. Did she speed up and attempt to break away from him? She would have tried, except for her earlier injury. Instead, she kept her eyes focussed straight ahead and tuned out the sounds around her.

By now, she surpassed the distances ran during her training. The muscles in her right calf burned, as did the ones in both her thighs. Lactic acid build-up. Great. She should have stopped at the water stations but was so intent on avoiding Zack Daniels, didn't bother. A long soak in a hot tub was in her future, along with a sports drink containing plenty of magnesium, and not necessarily in that order.

Her foot hurt. Blisters. Hilary pushed on through the burning pain. She pulled off the running surface when she could take the agony no more, sat down and removed her shoe. Blood soaked her sock in places. One spot, along the outside of her foot near her baby toe. The second on the back of her heel. Her instep pained like one of the bones in her foot was broken. All the training was for nothing. She couldn't finish the run.

Images of her time spent at the Terry Fox memorial flooded into her mind. He never gave up. Not until his cancer forced him. Her recollection was the inspiration she needed. Still, she had to contend with the mess her foot was in first.

Just her luck, Zack stopped and dropped to the ground beside her. "Looks nasty. Want some help?"

He was the last person she wanted to help her, but afraid of what sort of mess was under her bloody sock, she surrendered.

Zack slowly rolled her sock down to her ankle. Without speaking, he inched the stocking further. Hilary stiffened her leg and grimaced. She turned her head away and bit down on her lower lip when fabric and flesh separated from one another. At least the man was gentle and didn't yank them apart. Under her breath, she begged him not to use one of his pre-moistened first-aid wipes. This skin was rawer than her knee, and the alcohol would burn worse than the blisters.

"Give me some of your bandaids. I'll cover these for now, but they really need looking after."

She plucked a handful from her pocket and passed them to him. In minutes, he had her open blisters covered. When he applied the bandage near her baby toe, he pressed on the bottom of her foot. She grabbed her ankle and drew her extremity towards her knee. Another blister. At least this one didn't appear to be as severe as the others. It hadn't broken. She hauled the largest plaster from her pocket and covered this injury before Zack had her sock back in position.

"Thank you." What else could she say? She put her track shoe back on and readied herself to stand. Zack extended his hand. Reluctantly, she took it and pulled herself to her feet.

Farther down the path, a searing, stabbing stitch in her side stopped her in her tracks. Hilary pushed her hand into the painful location, hoping the action would bring her some comfort. No luck. Not even slow, deep breaths helped.

Zack drew beside her again. His helpful advice was uninvited and unwelcome. He opened his mouth to speak, and Hilary jogged away, despite the discomfort.

Tears burned her cheeks, but she was loathed to dash them away. She was within sight of the ten-kilometre finish line when she collapsed. So close, but she failed.

"It's not a race. It's a run. Stop and rest," Zack said.

Hilary tried to stand but immediately fell. She made a second attempt, but again, she was unsuccessful.

A lump formed in Erik's throat. He swallowed hard, but couldn't remove it. What felt like a hand squeezing his heart, sent a jolting pain through his chest. He started towards her, but a hand on his forearm stopped him.

"Don't. She won't thank you. Hilary's not a quitter. She'll finish what she started," said Luke. "I know. Tough seeing her like this. If it were Kim, I'd feel the same if she was out there."

The man was probably right. He knew Hilary better since he worked with her for ages. Erik only knew her for about eighteen months. There was more for him to learn about his fiancée. He sighed and blinked back tears.

Xena stamped her front feet like she was getting ready to run. A snap of his fingers and she settled.

A group of runners crossed the line, and Erik temporarily lost sight of Hilary. That was worse than seeing her struggle to return to her feet.

"Give me your hand, and I'll help you up," Zack said.

She shook her head.

"Don't be so stubborn, woman."

"I'll get up on my own if you don't mind."

Zack threw his hands in the air. "Fine then. I'll see you at the finish line." He jogged away, leaving Hilary to her own devices.

After he left, she regretted her stubbornness. She drew her knees to her chest and wrapped her arms around them. Her predicament required further thought.

Erik and Xena, Luke, Kim and their girls, and a few members of the force, waited for her at the finish line. Someone else joined them. A young boy and his mother. Rory! How did they know she was taking part in the race?

Hilary struggled to her feet and hobbled towards them. At that moment, Rory broke away from his mother and ran to her.

When he reached Hilary, he wrapped his arms around her waist and said, "I'll help you because you're like me."

With the assistance of the young boy, Hilary crossed the finish line.

Also by Melanie Robertson-King

The Consequences Collection
Tim's Magic Christmas
The Secret of Hillcrest House
A Shadow in the Past (second edition)
Shadows From Her Past
YESTERDAY TODAY ALWAYS
Cole's Notes (Revised version)
It Happened on Dufferin Terrace
All Aboard the Canadian with Buddy and his Four Fantastic
Furry Friends!
(King Park Press)

Cole's Notes (A Short Story)
EFD1: Starship Goodwords – a cross genre anthology
(CARRICK PUBLISHING, 2012)

Future Titles in the *It Happened* Series ...
featuring the Layne and Scott families

It Happened at Percé Rock

It Happened in Niagara Falls

It Happened at Lake Louise

MELANIE ROBERTSON-KING

https://melanierobertson-king.com

Melanie Robertson-King has always been a fan of the written word. Growing up as an only child, her face was almost always buried in a book from the time she could read. Her father was one of the thousands of Home Children sent to Canada through the auspices of The Orphan Homes of Scotland, and she has been fortunate to be able to visit her father's homeland many times and even met the Princess Royal (Princess Anne) at the orphanage where he was raised.